Letting go of earthly
possessions enables us
to take hold of
heavenly treasures.

—An Amish Proverb

# SUGARCREEK AMISH MYSTERIES

*Blessings in Disguise*
*Where Hope Dwells*
*The Buggy before the Horse*
*A Season of Secrets*
*O Little Town of Sugarcreek*
*Off the Beaten Path*
*Peace Like a River*
*Simply Vanished*
*A Stitch in Time*
*Mason Jar Mayhem*
*When There's a Will*
*Shoo, Fly, Shoo!*
*Earthly Treasures*

# EARTHLY
## Treasures

# ANNALISA DAUGHETY

**Guideposts**

New York

This book is dedicated with love to
my husband, Johnny Alliston.
You are the hero in my very own love story.
I am thankful for you and
what you've brought to my life.
You make everything more fun
(even cleaning out the chicken coop),
and I am so glad I get to do life with you.
You're my best friend and my partner—
and the best travel companion a girl could ask for.
I am looking forward to the future with you by my side
because with you, everything is an adventure.
I love you.

# Chapter One

Every August, Cheryl Cooper found herself struck by the urge to purchase school supplies. All those aisles of new crayons, pens, and blank notebooks were too tempting, despite the fact that she was several years removed from actually needing school supplies.

This year was no different.

"Do you have a little one headed back to school?" the cashier asked as she rang up a box of colored pencils.

Cheryl laughed. "No. It just seemed like a good time to stock up." She watched as the woman stuffed two boxes of crayons in a plastic bag. "And I'll donate some of this stuff to our local elementary school. I heard on the radio this morning that they'll be holding a school supply drive soon."

The woman grinned. "That's nice."

Cheryl paid and took her bags. Did she really look old enough to have kids in school? Of course she did. At thirty-one, she had many friends whose kids were either already in school or starting this year. What an odd thought. She was old enough to be someone's mom.

Sobered by the idea, she stepped out of the cool store and into the warm sunshine. Time seemed to be passing at the speed of light now that she'd hit her thirties.

She made her way to her car, still lost in thought until a piece of bright purple paper stuck under the windshield wiper blade of her car caught her eye. She pulled the paper off and glanced at it.

"It'll be a ton of fun."

Cheryl turned to see a young woman with jet black hair holding a stack of the purple flyers.

The young woman smiled. "Caught in the act." She held up the papers. "My boss is making me do this. Putting a flyer on every car in town isn't exactly my favorite thing." She sighed. "And seriously? I have no clue what I'm supposed to do about all the buggies."

"Leave the flyer with the horse?" Cheryl asked then grinned. "Kidding."

The woman giggled. "I know, right? I called him earlier today and made that very same remark. He said just to get it done. He wants the whole town to know about our event."

"What event is that?" Cheryl asked. She opened the door on her blue Ford Focus and tossed her purchases inside then turned back to face the woman.

"A geocaching slash treasure hunt." She made a slashing motion with one hand as she said it. "I'm Lori, by the way. Lori Groves."

"Nice to meet you. I'm Cheryl Cooper." She glanced down at the flyer that was in her hand. "Geocaching?"

"You ever heard of it?"

Cheryl thought for a moment. She at least knew the concept. "Yes. Hidden treasures are all over the country. And somehow you find them." She shrugged. "Maybe I'm not very clear on how to go about it."

Lori shook her head. "You're kinda right. At least you have the general idea." She set her giant stack of flyers on the hood of Cheryl's car. "You use GPS coordinates. Normally people log on to a Web site or use the geocaching app to find them. But in this case, they aren't typical caches."

"I'm not sure I follow."

"The geocaches on the Web site are always there. People find them and log the ones they find either on the paper that is with the cache or online."

"I've never understood what it is they find though."

Lori widened her smile. "Nothing big normally. And the general rule of thumb is that if you take something from the cache, you leave a treasure for the next hunter. You may find a coin and leave an eraser. Not a big prize, but still fun to hunt for something."

It might be the August heat, but it did sound appealing to Cheryl. "That sounds kind of fun."

"Oh, it is. Typically you sign your name and date on a little ledger that's with the hidden cache. It's fun to see all the people who've been there before you."

"So how is this going to work?" Cheryl held up the flyer.

"We've hidden some special geocaches. And there will be some other things hidden that are more like a scavenger hunt."

Cheryl skimmed over the flyer again. "Sounds interesting."

"Definitely. You should come to the big kickoff event we're hosting on Friday. I'll explain all the rules to everyone then—there's even a cash prize." Lori smiled. "All you need is a partner, and you'll be ready to join the hunt."

"Partner?" Cheryl asked.

"Yep. You'll work in teams. Believe me, you wouldn't want to try to solve some of the clues alone. They're kinda tricky." Lori tucked the stack of flyers under her arm. "I've got to run. I've got to visit a few businesses to see if I can leave stacks at their counters. But I hope to see you Friday evening. All the details are on there." She motioned toward Cheryl's flyer. "Tell your friends."

Cheryl said good-bye and climbed into her car. She was thankful the impromptu school supply run had been her last stop of the day. She'd been running errands ever since she'd placed the Closed sign on the door of the Swiss Miss. She couldn't wait to get home.

Home.

It had taken some time, but she thought of Sugarcreek as her home now. When her aunt Mitzi had left for Papua New Guinea to pursue a lifelong dream as a missionary, Cheryl—with a freshly broken heart and nothing important enough career-wise to keep her in Columbus—had uprooted her life and moved to Sugarcreek. She'd taken over as manager of her aunt's gift shop, the Swiss Miss, and had moved into Mitzi's adorable cottage.

Things had been shaky at first; in fact there had been times Cheryl had almost told Aunt Mitzi that the arrangement wasn't working. But soon she felt at home in quaint Sugarcreek and had made some wonderful friends.

She pulled into the driveway at the cottage and collected her things. As soon as she opened the door, her cell phone rang. She dropped her bags on the couch and fished her phone out of her purse.

"Hi, Momma." She sank on to the couch, and her cat, Beau, jumped into her lap. "What's up?" She'd just talked to her parents a few days before, a Sunday afternoon ritual they'd started when she'd first left home. "Is everything okay?"

"Is your guest room still ready for guests?" her mother asked.

Cheryl sat up. "Sure." Her parents had visited Sugarcreek a few months ago, but she'd love to see them again. "Why?"

"Do you remember your cousin Michelle? She's a bit older than you, but surely you remember her."

Cheryl thought for a moment. "Didn't she go to Ohio State? And her husband was on the football team there?"

"That's her. His name is Jared."

Michelle was about fifteen years older than Cheryl, so they hadn't been the sort of cousins who'd grown up together. "I guess I've sort of lost track of her now." Cheryl wondered if it made her an awful relative if she didn't even know for sure what state Michelle and her family lived in now. "Is she somewhere in Virginia?"

"They used to live in West Virginia years ago. But they've been near Cleveland for several years now. And she has a daughter who'll be a freshman at Ohio State this fall. Her name is Julia. I think you may have met her when she was a baby."

"That was many moons ago, Mom."

Her mother laughed. "Yes, I suppose it was. Anyway, apparently Julia has been wanting to visit Sugarcreek for a while. As Michelle put it, she has a slight obsession with all things Amish, and she'd love to come visit you for a couple of weeks."

"So I'd be responsible for a teenager?" Cheryl asked.

"She's going off to college in a few weeks, so it's not like she'll need a babysitter or anything. She's following her parents' footsteps and going to Ohio State. That's why she'll be traveling through your neck of the woods in the first place." Mom sighed. "I know it's asking a lot, but do you mind if she stays with you for about two weeks?"

Cheryl scratched Beau behind the ears. "What will we do?" She had babysat some in high school, but those had been little kids. She wasn't exactly equipped for life with a teenager.

Mom laughed. "You just do your normal stuff. Work, spend time with your friends there. Julia just needs a place to be her home base while she explores the area. She's an adult after all. Although…it would be nice if you took her sightseeing and maybe to one of those delicious restaurants nearby. I doubt she'll expect you or even want you to be with her 24–7."

"Okay, that sounds good."

"I'm glad, because I already told Michelle her daughter was welcome to stay."

Cheryl raked her fingers through her short red hair. She loved her mother, but sometimes the woman could drive her nuts. "Of course you did." She chuckled. "I am sure we'll have a lovely time."

"Michelle will be calling you any time now to make plans. I just wanted to give you a quick heads-up." She cleared her throat. "I think Julia will be arriving tomorrow. Michelle wasn't totally sure."

Tomorrow? Cheryl sighed. "Thanks, Momma. I love you. Tell Daddy I said hi and I love him too." They said their good-byes and hung up.

Cheryl rubbed Beau underneath his chin. "Seems like we'd better get ready for some company." So much for a quiet night at home with the book she'd checked out at the library.

She left Beau napping on the couch and went to see what kind of shape the guest room was in. It wasn't exactly pristine, but at least it wasn't too messy. She should have time to get the bedding washed while she ran to the grocery store.

Her phone dinged, signaling an incoming e-mail.

Aunt Mitzi.

The message was short and sweet.

Dearest Cheryl,

I'm having something of a crisis and need your assistance. I'll Skype you at 8:00 p.m. your time. Oh, Cheryl, I hope you get this and will be waiting on my call.

Much love,
Aunt Mitzi

Cheryl glanced at the clock. She had less than two hours until her aunt's call. She quickly stripped the guest bed and started the laundry as she imagined all the things that could be deemed a crisis on the mission field. Was her aunt sick? Had there been an accident? Was she in danger? Cheryl's mind raced.

Normally she wouldn't worry so much, but it wasn't like Aunt Mitzi to be so dramatic.

Cheryl said a quick prayer that everything was okay and headed out the door.

# Chapter Two

Promptly at eight, Cheryl was parked in front of her laptop. She'd raced through the grocery store, picking up a few items she felt would appeal to a teenage girl. The freshly laundered bedding was in place in the guest room, and she'd even dusted and vacuumed the room to make it feel more welcome.

The Skype ringtone sounded, and Cheryl hit Accept. For a moment the screen froze then Aunt Mitzi appeared.

"Good morning, Cheryl!" Aunt Mitzi said. "Or I guess I should say good evening." She grinned. In Papua New Guinea, it was midmorning on Thursday for Aunt Mitzi.

"Is everything okay?" Cheryl asked. "Are you sick?" She peered at the screen. Aunt Mitzi certainly didn't look sick. In fact, she looked radiant even through the fuzzy screen. Her cheeks were rosy.

Aunt Mitzi laughed. "I'm not sick." She quickly grew somber. "But I'm afraid I'm on shaky ground."

That didn't sound good. "What's wrong?"

"I need your advice." Aunt Mitzi pushed a wayward strand of gray hair from her face.

Cheryl wrinkled her nose. "Well that's a switch." She had a close relationship with her aunt, but for the most part, it had always been Aunt Mitzi dispensing advice to Cheryl. "What can I help you with?"

Aunt Mitzi looked sheepish. "I've been invited to a dinner."

"Oh. Well that's nice, right? Is it some kind of local thing?" Cheryl really admired her aunt for immersing herself in a new culture. Some kind of dinner event would definitely be a learning experience.

Aunt Mitzi sighed and shook her head. "No." She leaned closer to the screen. "There's a group here from Georgia, and they're doing some medical missions in the area. Part of the group is heading back, and they are having a send-off dinner in their honor."

"That sounds great." Her aunt had mentioned more than once that some of the conditions she encountered were pretty bad. "It seems like some basic medical help can really make a difference."

"You don't understand." Aunt Mitzi leaned in again and dropped her voice to a whisper. "A *man* invited me to go to the dinner. *With* him."

Cheryl widened her eyes. "Like a date?"

"I wouldn't call it a date. Not at my age." Aunt Mitzi looked worried. "Would you?"

Cheryl grinned. She was pretty sure dating had no real age limits. "Do you want it to be a date?"

"That's just it. I don't know. I never pictured myself in this position." Aunt Mitzi had dreamed for years of doing mission work, but her husband hadn't shared the same dream. They'd had a wonderful life together in Sugarcreek until he passed away a few years ago after forty years of marriage. As far as Cheryl knew, she hadn't so much as had coffee with a man since his death. "I guess I never thought about it."

"Does he have a name?"

A smile spread across Aunt Mitzi's face. "Ted. He's a retired doctor and a widower. He's planning to stay here after the team heads back home. He says his dream has always been to spend some time doing medical missions, and he's finally at the point in his life where he can."

Cheryl thought it sounded precious and promising, but she didn't say that to her aunt. Two like-minded people at similar points in life, serving the Lord together. What could be better? "Well, what's your holdup?"

"I don't want to lose my focus. I didn't come here to socialize or to focus on myself." Aunt Mitzi frowned. "He's a very nice man though, and I think we may have some things in common."

"It might be good to have a friend."

"Yes. That would be nice. A friend." Aunt Mitzi brightened. "Maybe you're right."

"So you'll go?" Cheryl asked.

"I'll consider it."

Cheryl chuckled. She could see how torn her aunt was. "I don't think you should feel guilty for wanting to go to a dinner and have a fun time. Everyone needs a break sometimes. You work hard there. And I know there are times it's lonely and challenging. If you want my advice, I think you should take a night off and go have dinner with the group from Georgia. Including Ted the retired doctor."

"Thanks for your input." Mitzi sat up straighter. "I'm sorry for sounding so frantic on the e-mail. It just shocked me when he invited me, and I'm afraid I didn't know what to say or do."

"That's okay."

"Tell me what's going on there."

Cheryl quickly filled her aunt in on the little she knew about the upcoming treasure hunt.

"That sounds so exciting. Who will be your partner?"

Cheryl hesitated. She already had a partner in mind but had no idea if Levi Miller would even consider participating in something like that. The Amish man and his family had become great friends to Cheryl. "I'm not sure. I guess I'll decide this week though."

Aunt Mitzi gave her a knowing look but kept quiet. That was the trouble with Skype. Even without her saying a word, she knew what her aunt was thinking. "Give my best to Naomi and her family," Aunt Mitzi said pointedly. Naomi Miller was Levi's stepmother and one of Cheryl's best friends in Sugarcreek. "And keep me posted."

"I will. And I have a houseguest arriving tomorrow." She explained about Julia's upcoming visit. Just as her mom had predicted, Michelle had called while Cheryl was on the way to the grocery store to confirm the trip. "I just hope Sugarcreek is entertaining enough for a teenage girl."

"Oh, she'll love it." Aunt Mitzi smiled. "My laptop battery is getting low. I think we'd better end the call."

Cheryl nodded. "E-mail me if you get the chance. I want to know how things go."

"I will."

They said their good-byes, and Cheryl closed the laptop. So Aunt Mitzi might have a suitor. There was something so hopeful about the situation. It was just like Cheryl's grandma used to say— no matter what stage of life you were in, God might have a surprise in store around the next corner.

Thursday morning, just as Cheryl was about to unlock the door to the Swiss Miss, she heard her name from across the street. She looked over and saw Kathy Snyder waving to her. She set Beau's cat carrier down on the sidewalk in front of the store and walked across the street.

Kathy met her on the sidewalk in front of her shop, a smile on her face. "Have you heard about the big treasure hunt that's coming to Sugarcreek?"

Cheryl nodded. "Yesterday I met the woman who seems to be in charge."

"Dark hair and handing out purple flyers?" Kathy asked.

"Yep. That's her. It looks kind of fun, doesn't it?"

"I've heard lots of buzz about it in the café." She chuckled. "Get it? Buzz?"

Cheryl grinned. The Honey Bee Café was one of Cheryl's favorite places for lunch and the added bonus was getting to chat with Kathy. The two of them had become friends over the past year, and Cheryl felt like they could discuss just about anything. "Funny. I think I'll plan to go to the information meeting. My cousin's daughter will be getting to town sometime today, and that sounds like something entertaining to take her to."

"How old is she?" Kathy asked.

"She just graduated from high school, so I'm guessing around eighteen. She's going to be a freshman at Ohio State in a couple of weeks."

"Is she just coming to visit you?"

Cheryl shrugged. "Apparently she's interested in visiting Amish country. I don't know much else about her, but I guess I will soon."

Kathy nodded. "Sounds like fun. I'm planning to be at the treasure hunt kickoff too, so maybe I'll see you guys there."

"You might see us before then," Cheryl said. "There's a good chance we'll be over to eat."

They said good-bye, and Cheryl hurried into the Swiss Miss to go through the process of opening for the day. One thing she'd come to love were her morning rituals.

She slipped on her cheery red Swiss Miss apron. Naomi had made them for store employees so they would be easily recognizable to customers. They had the store name embroidered on the front on a cute white heart.

Naomi was very involved with things at the Swiss Miss and had been a good friend to Aunt Mitzi before Cheryl's arrival. She provided homemade baked goods for the store, and her teenage daughter, Esther, worked in the Swiss Miss part-time. Another Amish teenager, Lydia Troyer, also worked in the store part-time, but she was taking some time off this month.

Beau tangled himself around her feet, his way of telling her it was time for his breakfast. Once she'd poured a scoop of food in his bowl, she tidied up the counter area.

Just as Aunt Mitzi had done, Cheryl always made it a practice to open the Swiss Miss early for locals. It wasn't unusual for other business owners to stop in for a loaf of Naomi's homemade bread or some of Katie's homemade buttercream fudge. Oftentimes the Vogel brothers, Rueben and Ben, stopped by for an early morning game of checkers.

The Vogels had intrigued Cheryl ever since she'd first arrived in Sugarcreek. When she'd first met them, they hardly spoke. One had remained in the Amish faith and the other had left years ago. The brothers maintained a strained relationship since, but over the past year Cheryl had observed them interacting more with one another. It was nice to watch their relationship change for the better.

The bell above the Swiss Miss door jingled, and Naomi Miller stepped inside, a basket of what Cheryl hoped was homemade bread in her hand. "*Guder mariye*," she said with a smile.

Although the Amish woman was a decade older than Cheryl, her petite size and smooth skin often made Cheryl forget the age difference. "How are you today?" Cheryl asked.

"I am doing well. I am sorry I did not make it by yesterday with the bread." She held up the basket. "I was tied up with making one of the last batches of the summer strawberry preserves."

"In that case, it's no problem." Cheryl grinned. "I'm pretty sure any weight I've gained over the past year can be attributed to your homemade bread and strawberry preserves." Not to mention Naomi's products were best-selling items for the Swiss Miss.

Naomi put the basket on the counter. "Levi will bring the preserves by the store tomorrow." Naomi had married Levi's father,

Seth, when Levi was young. Seth's first wife, Ruth, had died during the birth of Levi's sister, Sarah.

Cheryl felt the familiar butterflies at the mention of Levi. Would she always have a reaction to simply hearing his name? "That's great. Thanks."

She filled Naomi in on her upcoming houseguest as well as the treasure hunt. "I have already seen a flyer about that," Naomi said with a smile. "It sounds like an interesting event. I cannot help but wonder who is hosting the hunt and why they chose Sugarcreek."

The same thought had crossed Cheryl's mind last night. "Maybe you and Seth can attend the opening meeting on Friday. They will be explaining how it works, and I'm sure the host of the event will be there. Yesterday Lori kept referring to her boss. I guess he is the one behind the whole thing."

"Seth is a busy man, but perhaps I can persuade him to attend with me." Naomi smiled. "And I am looking forward to meeting your guest."

Cheryl frowned. "Julia's mother told me she is interested in Amish country. I certainly hope she won't bug you with questions and such." Now that she lived among the Amish and considered Naomi and Levi some of her closest friends, she was fiercely protective of them. She wanted no one—not even her younger cousin—to make them feel uncomfortable.

But Naomi dismissed her worries with a laugh. "It will be fine. I am sure Julia's visit will be a joy to all of us."

Cheryl hoped so. And she supposed later that night she would find out.

# CHAPTER THREE

Cheryl paced the living room. It was nearly ten and much later than she'd expected Julia to arrive. She'd gone back and forth about when to call Michelle and had finally decided on ten sharp.

Just as she was reaching for the phone, there was a knock at the door.

She opened it, and a striking red-haired girl stood on the step.

"Julia! Come in. I was beginning to get worried."

Julia, clad in a dark green bohemian-style dress, stepped inside and set her oversized shoulder bag next to the couch. "Sorry. Thanks for letting me crash here for a few weeks." She smiled, and Cheryl was struck again by how pretty she was. Her red hair was a darker shade than Cheryl's, and instead of freckles, she had creamy skin with a hint of a summer tan.

"No problem. I'm glad to have you." Cheryl closed the door. "Do you have more bags in the car that I can help you with?"

Julia shook her head. "Not tonight. I'll bring my other suitcase in tomorrow. No biggie."

Cheryl was suddenly aware of the potential awkwardness of the situation. A houseguest who was a relative, whom she'd never had an actual conversation with—except for perhaps a game of patty-cake when Julia was a baby. This could be a bad idea. "Can I get you something to eat or drink?"

"I'd love some hot tea if you have it."

"I sure do. Follow me." Cheryl led her into the kitchen and pointed out the varieties she had available.

"Chamomile is great. It always helps me sleep." Julia smiled. "I can make it though. I don't want you to go to any trouble."

Cheryl gestured to the kitchen table. "No trouble. Have a seat, and I'll make both of us a cup. Did you have an eventful trip?"

"Not really. I left a little later than I meant to. My boyfriend, Trevor, wanted to take me out for supper."

"That's nice. Will he be at school with you at Ohio State?" Cheryl put a pot of water on the stove to boil and pulled two mugs out of the cabinet.

"Yes. I'll see him again when we move into the dorms."

Cheryl dropped a tea bag in each mug. "What made you decide to take a road trip before school?" She remembered those weeks before she'd gone off to college. She'd soaked up every moment with her family and high school friends that she could.

Julia shrugged. "We didn't do any kind of vacation this year because I spent the summer working. I just decided that I'd like to get out and see something new. I'd heard about you living here and thought it might be okay to stay. Thanks for letting me."

Cheryl put a mug of tea in front of her. "There's sugar on the table." She grinned. "I tend to be a little heavy on the sugar, so it might be best for you to do your own." She sat down across from

Julia. "Is there anything in particular you want to see or do while you're here?"

Julia took a sip of tea. "There are a couple of cheese factories I want to visit. And I'm hoping you can point me toward a farmers' market or something like that."

"The foodie tour," Cheryl said. "That sounds good. I can definitely give you directions to those things. And if you're interested in authentic Amish cooking, there are some delicious restaurants around."

"Sounds wonderful."

"So are you excited about heading off to school?" Cheryl remembered the transition to college as being one of the most exciting times of her life.

A cloud passed across Julia's face, but it was almost instantly replaced by a smile. "I am. It will be so much fun to be on my own. I'll be a legacy in the sorority my mom was in if I decide to go through rush. And I'm majoring in marketing—they have a great program. I think it will be so cool to be surrounded by such a variety of people from such diverse backgrounds."

"Sounds amazing." Cheryl couldn't help but think that Julia sounded a lot like a college brochure. "How about Trevor? Is he excited?"

"Yeah. He's going to be an accountant just like my dad and his dad. They work together." She frowned. "Trevor already knows his roommate—it's a guy we were in school with. But my best friend is going to school out of state. So I figured I'd just leave it up to chance."

That was a brave move. Living in a tiny dorm room with someone she'd never met sounded pretty awful to Cheryl. "Have you been paired up with someone yet?"

"Yeah. Some girl named Audrey from Canton." She sighed. "Mom thinks I should apply for a private room until I pledge and then live in the sorority house like she did, but I'm not sure."

"It's a lot to figure out," Cheryl admitted.

"I'll be glad when things have settled and everything is figured out," Julia said.

Cheryl wondered if she should warn the younger girl that truthfully things were never settled. Life was full of changes, and sometimes even when you think you have things figured out, they have a way of changing. But she'd save that talk for another day. "You're welcome to go with me to the Swiss Miss tomorrow if you'd like."

"I think I might like to sleep in a little if that's okay. Then I'll go explore."

"Suit yourself." She rinsed her mug out in the sink and put it in the dishwasher. "Please make yourself at home while you're here."

Julia followed suit. "Thanks."

Cheryl introduced her to Beau and showed her where the guest room, bathroom, and towels were.

"This place is so cute," Julia said.

"Thanks. A lot of it is Aunt Mitzi's style, but now that I've been here for a year, I've started to put some of my own décor in the place." Cheryl wanted the cottage to feel welcoming and cozy, and so far it did. Since Aunt Mitzi hadn't really given her an end date to how long she'd be away, it was hard for Cheryl to know what was too much or too little to do as far as making the place her own.

"It's a great mix of styles." Julia yawned. "I'll see you tomorrow. Thanks again for letting me stay."

"No problem."

Cheryl sank into her bed. Julia was a sweet girl. In fact, she sort of reminded Cheryl of herself when she'd been eighteen.

After a fitful sleep where she dreamed she and Julia were the same age, Cheryl hurriedly started her Friday. She'd heard that a good-sized tour group was coming in today by bus, and those were always busy days for the shop.

She and Beau left the house quietly. Julia hadn't stirred yet. She would text her later and see how things were going.

Once she had the store up and going, Cheryl sank on to a stool. She probably had a few minutes before customers began arriving. She glanced down at the treasure hunt flyer she'd left on the counter. There didn't appear to be an entry fee to participate. If Levi didn't want to be her partner, maybe Julia would.

The bell above the door jingled, and Cheryl looked up.

Levi Miller strode into the store, a box of Naomi's strawberry jam in his arms. "Guder mariye, Cheryl."

Cheryl grinned. "Hey, Levi. How are you today?"

"Things are good. The petting zoo is keeping me busy." The Millers operated a petting zoo and offered buggy rides on their farm. It was a popular activity with the many visitors to Sugarcreek.

"I'll have to be sure to bring my cousin's daughter out for a visit. I think she'd enjoy seeing the farm." She filled Levi in on Julia's visit.

He glanced at the flyer in front of her. "*Maam* told me about the treasure hunt. It sounds interesting."

Cheryl froze. Now was the time to ask him to be her partner. She wished she'd rehearsed what to say. She didn't want it to seem like she was asking him on a date or anything. "They're having a kickoff meeting tonight where they'll explain how the hunt works, and I think they'll serve refreshments."

"I wonder how many people will participate."

"I'm not sure. Yesterday I talked to Kathy Snyder, and she says there's a buzz around town about the hunt." Heat rose up her face as she prepared to ask him. "They're wanting people to sign up in teams. Pairs, actually."

"Oh?" Levi took his hat off and ran his fingers through his blond hair.

"I was wondering… Well… I thought maybe…" She was horrible at this. "Would you want to be on a team with me? You know Sugarcreek and the surrounding area so much better than I do."

Levi grinned. "That does sound fun. I am not sure how much extra time I have though, with work and all."

Her heart sank.

"But if we can hunt for treasure after work, I think I would be available." His blue eyes twinkled. "Who knows? Maybe we will win."

She felt twenty pounds lighter. "Thanks. Yes, that sounds good. I guess I'll see you at the kickoff then?"

"I will be there." Levi tipped his hat and walked out of the store.

Cheryl couldn't keep the grin off her face. She already felt like she'd won, and they hadn't even started the competition.

A tour group arrived soon after Levi left, and Cheryl was busy till lunchtime. As the last of the tourists left the shop, packages in hand, Esther Miller came in.

"It looks like you have been busy," she said, tying on her apron over her plain dress.

When Cheryl first met Esther, she'd been in *rumspringa*. The tradition in the Amish faith literally meant "running around," and it had surprised Cheryl. As Naomi had explained, it was a time for Amish young people to explore the outside world and decide if they would remain Amish and join the church or leave the faith they'd grown up in.

Esther had recently decided to join the church, and she'd given up the jeans and T-shirts of rumspringa and replaced them with simple Amish dresses and an always present prayer *kapp*.

"It was a busy morning," Cheryl admitted. "It seems like quilts were the rage with this group. And Levi's leather Bible covers sold well too." Naomi wasn't the only member of the Miller family to contribute items to the Swiss Miss. Levi made beautiful leather Bible covers that were very popular.

"I think he is planning to make more," Esther said. "But you know how busy he is."

Cheryl nodded. "I know." She glanced at the clock. "Can you watch the store while I run home for lunch?" She'd texted Julia earlier and the girl had said she was fine, but Cheryl wanted to check on her to be sure. She might like to have lunch or something.

Esther nodded. "*Ja*. Take your time. I'll be fine."

Cheryl tucked her apron behind the counter, gave Beau a pat on the head, and headed out into the beautiful day. She loved living close enough to work to be able to walk—although when it was very cold she sometimes drove.

She arrived at the cottage, and Julia's vehicle was gone. Oh well. At least Cheryl could grab a bite to eat. She unlocked the door and tossed her purse on the couch. In the kitchen, she took the ingredients for a salad out of the fridge. Today was a day to eat healthy because she knew with company in town, they'd probably eat out for dinner a few times.

She went to grab her library book from her room and noticed a folded piece of paper on the floor of the hallway. She unfolded it.

The Ohio State logo was on top. She scanned the paper. It was a scholarship offer addressed to Julia.

And she'd checked the "decline" box.

Cheryl replaced the paper exactly the way she'd found it and walked away, her mind reeling.

# CHAPTER FOUR

Later that afternoon, Cheryl still hadn't decided how to handle the situation. Julia and Michelle had both mentioned how pleased they were by the great scholarship Ohio State had offered. So why decline it?

She paced the quilt aisle at the Swiss Miss. There was no reason to think there was anything wrong. Julia was obviously excited about college. Perhaps she'd been offered a better scholarship than the one on the paper in the hallway. Either way, it wasn't really Cheryl's business unless Julia or Michelle mentioned it.

Right?

The bell above the Swiss Miss door rang, and Naomi stepped inside.

"Whew." She hurried down the aisle to the counter. "I think we must be having a heat wave."

Cheryl chuckled and took in the Amish woman's flushed cheeks. "It appears so."

Naomi grinned. "You can remind me of this complaining when I am out doing chores in the snow this winter."

Cheryl nodded. "I'll remember that." She sighed.

"Is everything okay?" Naomi asked.

Cheryl filled her in on the declined scholarship form she'd found in the hallway. "Do I mention it? Or do I wait and see if she brings it up?"

Naomi was quiet for a moment. "I have found that sometimes with my own children, talking to them about the subject in question sometimes gives them an opening to bring up any concerns or issues they are having."

"That seems like a good strategy. Maybe tonight at dinner I can just bring up her upcoming move-in day at school. Hopefully from there, she'll let me know if there's anything going on— particularly if there is something her parents don't yet know."

"Is that what worries you?"

Cheryl shrugged. "I barely know them. But Julia is a guest in my home, and although she's legally an adult, I feel very responsible for her while she's here. However, I'm not sure it's my place to meddle in things, especially if I don't know all the facts."

"Sounds like you have it figured out then." Naomi smiled. "You are much wiser than you give yourself credit for, Cheryl. I will be praying that you handle the situation in the best way possible."

Ever since she'd moved to Sugarcreek, Naomi had regularly let her know she was praying for her in various situations. It always calmed Cheryl and gave her such a sense of peace. Cheryl knew God heard her prayers, but having Naomi also praying on her behalf meant so much. "Thank you."

"I stopped by to let you know that Seth and I will be in attendance tonight at the kickoff meeting. That is not to say Seth will actually participate, but he is curious enough to attend." She smiled.

"That will be fun. I'm anxious to find out the details." She was also anxious to see if Levi would really find time to be her partner, but she didn't want to mention that to Naomi.

Once Naomi was gone, Cheryl began tidying up. Fridays in late summer were normally pretty busy, but after the morning tour bus rush, this afternoon had been slow. Cheryl scooped up Beau and placed him gently in the carrier. It was time to call it a day.

She walked home at a leisurely pace. The leaves were just beginning to change, and in spite of Naomi's declaration that there was a late summer heat wave upon them, Cheryl was convinced she felt a hint of fall in the afternoon air. Last fall she'd been a newcomer to Sugarcreek. She'd arrived in town not really knowing anyone and had been forced by her breakup with Lance to reimagine the life she'd planned.

Now she had found a place for herself in the quaint town. She no longer felt like just a temporary fill-in for Aunt Mitzi, but someone who really belonged. That's not to say she wasn't sometimes plagued with the nagging questions about what she'd do when Aunt Mitzi decided to return from the mission field. The cottage she lived in was her aunt's, and even though she'd made herself at home, it had crossed her mind that it might not be a forever home.

Those worries could wait though, perhaps for a day when Aunt Mitzi was home on furlough and they could discuss the future face-to-face.

For now though, she planned to stay focused on the present. There was no point in worrying about what the future may or may not hold, especially not on a beautiful Friday afternoon.

She rounded the corner to the cottage. Julia's car was parked in the driveway. She'd tried to call earlier but hadn't gotten an answer.

"It's just me," she called as she opened the door. She set the cat carrier on the floor and opened it. Beau paused long enough to rub against her legs before he scurried off.

"I'm in the kitchen," Julia said.

Cheryl walked into the kitchen, and her eyes widened. The kitchen counters were covered in bowls, baking sheets, and ingredients. Julia was in the process of mixing something in a large red bowl. "Wow. It looks like you've been busy."

Julia laughed. "I thought I'd make dinner." She poured the bowl's contents into a waiting pie crust. "And dessert." She grinned. "A simple apple pie."

"It doesn't look so simple to me." Cheryl could do basic things in the kitchen, but she'd never be one of those people remembered fondly for her cooking. "But you didn't have to go to this trouble. I was going to take you out to dinner tonight and show you some of the culinary delights Sugarcreek has to offer."

"Oh, that would've been nice. But this is no trouble for me. In fact, it's kind of how I unwind." Julia grinned. "I know that's weird, but I've always been happiest in the kitchen. My parents are on this crazy no-carb, low-fat diet so I don't get to cook as much as I'd like at home. Cooking for one just isn't as fun."

Cheryl knew all too well what she meant. "That's very true. A lot of times I just get takeout instead of cooking a whole meal just for myself. After about the second day of leftovers, my taste buds are ready for something new." She gestured around the kitchen. "This is amazing though. I really appreciate it."

Julia beamed. "No problem. Dinner will be ready in about half an hour, and the pie should be done by the time we're through eating the main course. And don't worry. I'll get all of this cleaned up."

Sure enough, by the time Cheryl had changed into jeans and fixed her hair and makeup, the kitchen was spotless. She sat down at the table. "This looks and smells amazing. What is it?"

Julia giggled. "This is a recipe that's one of my favorites. It's a citrus chicken marinated in garlic and chilies. I think you'll love it." She took the lid off a Pyrex dish. "Served with a side of rosemary mashed potatoes, also one of my favorites." She removed another lid. "And baby carrots with a maple glaze." She grinned. "And apple pie for dessert, but you've already seen that."

Cheryl's mouth watered. "I'm impressed." She was even more impressed once she'd had a few bites. "This is delicious."

"Thanks." Julia ate in silence for a moment. "I'm just glad you're not on some crazy diet like my mom and dad. Trevor likes to eat, but usually he'd rather go out to dinner than stay home and have something home-cooked."

"That will change someday when he gets older. Believe me. Never underestimate the value of a home-cooked meal." Cheryl took a bite of chicken that was a perfect blend of sweet citrus and tangy chilies. "Maybe we should go have dinner at my friend Naomi's house sometime while you're here. She's Amish, and her food is seriously to die for."

"I'd like that. I've tried a few Amish recipes before, but it would be cool to eat in an Amish home."

"You'll meet Naomi and some of her family tonight at the scavenger hunt kickoff event." Cheryl finished the last bite of her potatoes. "It should be a fun time."

Julia got up and took the pie out of the oven. "Are you ready for dessert?"

"Always." Cheryl chuckled. "Make mine a small slice though."

Julia obliged. "Here you go." She placed the steaming pie in front of Cheryl. "This is kind of my go-to dessert."

Cheryl took a small bite and smiled. "This is incredible."

"I found fresh apples at that farmers' market you gave me directions to. Fresh ingredients like that make such a huge difference in how recipes taste. A recipe might be good with store-bought ingredients, but if I'm able to purchase freshly picked and locally grown ingredients, it's even better."

"You really know your stuff." Cheryl was impressed. At first glance, Julia looked like a typical teenager, but she seemed so much more grown up than Cheryl had expected. "Remind me again how old you are."

Julia chuckled. "I'll be nineteen in a couple of months. I was always the oldest in my class. I used to wish my parents had gone ahead and sent me to kindergarten a year earlier, but now I'm glad things turned out this way."

"That makes sense. I remember a kid in my class that was the opposite—she started kindergarten when she was still four, almost five. When we all turned sixteen and got our licenses, she was miserable because she wouldn't get hers until the next school year had already begun."

"Yeah, I was definitely better off, but I guess now I'm sort of more eager to get out on my own than maybe I would be otherwise."

"And as an only child, I'll bet that goes over really well with your parents."

A shadow crossed Julia's face. "They're not especially happy with letting me go. But they want what's best for me, so they aren't being too sappy about it."

Now was her chance to dig. "And I'm sure with the great scholarship you're getting from Ohio State, it's a little easier for them to let go some."

Julia shrugged. "I guess. They were pumped when the offer came in and took Trevor and me out to a fancy restaurant to celebrate. But we've known that's where I was going to go to school pretty much since I was born. We have pictures of me as a toddler in a little Buckeyes' cheerleading uniform. It wasn't even a question when it came time to apply to schools."

"It's nice that you've found a place you know you'll belong." Julia hadn't even flinched at the mention of the scholarship. So maybe she should chalk the whole thing up to some kind of misunderstanding. "Those college years can be a tough transition."

"That's what I keep hearing." Julia smiled. "But I'm ready to see for myself."

Cheryl took her pie plate and fork to the sink. "In about two weeks, I guess you will." It didn't seem like that long ago that Cheryl herself was moving into the dorm.

"I can't believe the time is already here," Julia said. "One minute I was a little girl headed to kindergarten, and the next one I was crossing the stage at graduation."

Cheryl could identify with the sentiment. "Time definitely seems to pass faster the older you get. Just wait till you hit your thirties. Sometimes it feels as if life has accidentally gotten stuck in fast-forward." Each passing year seemed to speed by even quicker than the last one.

"I'm not sure if it makes me feel better that I'm not the only one, or worse that apparently you blink and you're gray."

Cheryl couldn't hide her smile. The whole "time passes quickly" thing had been one of life's hardest lessons for her. "That's not what I meant. It's not like I don't have wonderful memories of the years since high school. But now that I'm in my thirties, I've learned to embrace each moment a little more. I hope you'll get up each day with the knowledge that you don't get another day just like that again. Even the stinky Mondays when you're out of coffee and running late."

Julia grinned. "Gotcha. I think I can do that. I guess we should all be living that way anyway, right? I mean, we're not promised tomorrow."

Wisdom from the eighteen-year-old. It was a concept most teens hadn't exactly grasped. Cheryl remembered the days of feeling invincible. When the first of her classmates had passed away in an accident, the reality of how brief life could be had hit the entire class. "No, we're not. That's why it's important to live each day to the fullest." She grinned and scooped up another slice of pie with her fork. "And always have dessert."

# CHAPTER FIVE

That night Cheryl and Julia made their way to the bleachers at the local park where the other scavenger hunt participants sat eagerly waiting. "There are some of my friends. We can sit with them." She led Julia to where Seth, Naomi, and Levi sat. A few rows above them, Kathy Snyder waved.

"Julia, this is Seth, Naomi, and Levi Miller."

The Millers greeted Julia.

"It is so nice to meet you," Levi said.

Julia smiled. "Thank you."

They took their seats, and Cheryl looked around at the competition. She spotted several people in the crowd whom she didn't recognize. Before she could ask Naomi if she knew who they were, Lori made her way to the front of the crowd.

"Welcome, everyone," she said. "We are so excited about this treasure hunt that's taking place in Sugarcreek over the next two weeks. I'm Lori Groves, and I'm here on behalf of my boss, Mr. Andrew Arnold. He wasn't able to make it tonight, but he will be arriving in Sugarcreek soon and he's looking forward to meeting each of you." She paused behind the podium. "Let me explain how this competition is going to work," she said. "You'll sign up in teams of two. If there's an odd man out who wants to join a two-person team, that's okay, but let's try to make three the limit."

The crowd nodded.

"Has anyone ever heard of geocaching?" she asked.

A few people raised their hands. Cheryl had read about it once but never tried it.

"Most people don't know this, but there are hidden treasures all across the land in the form of geocaches. There are apps and Web sites you can use that will help you locate any geocache hidden in a certain area. Sometimes there's a riddle to solve to find the location and sometimes it's strictly done on GPS coordinates. Since I'm aware that some of our participants won't have smartphones with them, we're going to rely solely on riddles. So this won't be a traditional geocaching hunt but more of a hybrid." She grinned.

Cheryl was impressed that she knew her audience. If any of the Amish townspeople participated—and judging by the number of them she saw in the audience, they would—they would be at a disadvantage if a smartphone was required.

"What you're looking for, though, will definitely be like a traditional geocache. For those of you who've never hunted for one before, you're likely looking for a sturdy, waterproof container of some sort. It will be hidden out of sight. Once you locate the box, open it. Now if this were a regular geocaching hunt, inside you'd find a trinket of some sort. A coin, a pencil, a small figurine...something like that. If you take a treasure, you have to be prepared to leave one in its place." She grinned. "But in this competition, you won't have to worry about that. What you need will already be waiting for you inside the box."

A hand went up in the front. "What will be in there?" a man asked.

"For one, a ledger. You'll sign your names in the order you find the box. Don't worry about anyone cheating." Her eyes twinkled mischievously. "There is a motion-sensing camera hidden near the site. It will help me ensure I know the order the competitors arrived."

"That's pretty cool," Julia whispered.

"Once you sign the names of you and your partner, look inside the box. There you'll find an envelope with your names on it. Take the envelope, and inside you'll find your next clue."

The audience murmured excitedly.

"However, you won't be able to immediately go out and find the next place. The clue will tell you when it's available for hunting." She looked around. "Does anyone have any questions so far?"

Kathy Snyder raised her hand. "Are the clues related in any way? I mean, is there a theme or something to be aware of?"

"Great question," Lori said with a smile. "But no. The only thing they have in common is that they are all within a certain radius of Sugarcreek." She walked over to a table and lifted a stack of papers. "I have maps here for everyone. Nothing will be hidden outside of the parameters of the map. That's the one thing you can be certain of. But the clues themselves aren't related to each other and don't build on each other to find the next one." She stepped back to the podium. "There will be two clues in the first round. Tuesday night at seven in this same spot, we'll have a second meeting. At that time, I'll announce the five teams who are moving on."

The crowd chattered. "How do you know who the top five will be?" an older lady asked. "How do you calculate that?"

"The five teams who arrived to the two locations with the best overall times. Imagine a stopwatch starting at the time the clue opens. However many minutes it runs before each team checks in for that day will be their score. So if the clue opens at 10:00 a.m. and your team arrives at 10:45, your score will be forty-five. If the second clue opens at 1:00 p.m. and you get there at 3:45, your score for that day will be one hundred and sixty-five. We'd add those two numbers together to have your total score for the first two clues. The top five teams will move on. If there's a tie in the overall scores, we'll allow for more teams to move on." She glanced around. "Does anyone have any questions about the way the scoring works?"

Cheryl thought for a moment. The way Lori had explained it made sense. It would be like an invisible timer began running when the clues opened and wouldn't stop for each team until they located the box and signed the ledger. Of course, she suspected the motion cameras would likely give Lori the exact times of arrival. That made it impossible to cheat. It seemed like a good system.

"So neither clue is more important than the other?" asked a young guy sitting in the row above Cheryl.

"Right. They all have equal billing. So even if you have a longer time than you'd like in finding the first one, you may be really fast on the second one. You never know how long it will take the other teams." She smiled. "Of course, you'll be able to gauge your success somewhat when you sign the logbook. If there are ten teams ahead of you on the first clue and fifteen ahead of you on the second clue, it's pretty safe to assume you won't move on."

The crowd nodded along.

"The final five teams will move on to the second round. They'll hunt for three more clues. I'll give the third clue out on Tuesday night when I announce the final teams. The fourth and fifth clues will be found as you move through the competition. I must warn you though—the clues will get harder as we go. When the hunt is over, there will be a final wrap-up party and the winning team will be announced." She grinned. "There's one final item, and I think this is the most exciting part." She paused dramatically. "There will be a one-thousand-dollar cash prize to the winning team at the end of the competition."

Several people in the crowd gasped.

Cheryl and Levi exchanged a glance. A thousand dollars was a lot of money.

"So now that you know the grand prize, I hope you'll pair up and join the hunt. I'll be here to answer any questions you may have. Otherwise, choose your partner and come down to the registration table to sign up. You'll get your map and the first clue when you do." She smiled. "But for those of you who are extra curious, I'll go ahead and read it now." She took a slip of paper from the table and cleared her throat. "Here's the clue:

"Nothing is planted
in this garden of stone.

This city is silent

so you may feel alone.

High up on a hill

and shrouded in mystery,

there you'll find statues

and some interesting history."

Lori grinned. "This clue will be open for hunting at ten o'clock tomorrow morning. I hope to see all of you back here on Tuesday." She dismissed the crowd and made her way to the registration table. People were already lining up to register.

"What do you think?" she asked Levi as they stood.

He smiled. "It sounds like she is going to accommodate people who work during the day. I think we should sign up." He frowned. "Unless you think your cousin wants to be your partner."

"I asked her earlier, and she said she didn't think she wanted to do it. She's not familiar with Sugarcreek, and I think she's happy to just play tourist." She glanced over at Naomi and Seth. "Do you want to see if Naomi wants to sign up on our team?"

He nodded. "Ja. That is a *goot* idea. I do not think *Daed* will do it, and I think she wants to see what it is all about."

Cheryl followed Levi out of the bleachers and made her way to where Seth and Naomi stood. "Naomi, would you like to sign up with Levi and me?" she asked. "We can have a team of three."

Naomi's eyes sparkled. "Thank you for asking, Cheryl. I do not believe I will sign up, but I would like to go with you on one of the hunts." She grinned. "You and I have been reprimanded so many times for playing detective. This gives us a chance to do so with no danger involved."

Cheryl chuckled. "True."

"You two will definitely have an advantage over the competition after all your experience seeking out clues," Seth said. "At least this time I will not have to remind you that you are not real detectives." He smiled at his wife. "Or worry about your safety."

Naomi nodded. "That is true, Husband. Our clue hunting will be perfectly harmless." She grinned. "I will leave most of the hunting to Levi and Cheryl though. Perhaps I will join in on the second clue. The two of you will do fine without me I am sure." She cast what could be considered a knowing glance at Cheryl.

Cheryl's cheeks grew hot. "Well, we'll love to have you whenever you're available."

Levi turned to Julia. "You too. If you want to sign up and join us, please do."

Julia shook her head. "That's kind, but I'm going to be kind of on my own schedule these next few weeks. Pretty soon I'll have nearly every waking moment scheduled for me. I'm going to enjoy these few days of freedom while they last."

These were really the last days of true freedom Julia would have, but Cheryl didn't want to point that out. She remembered being in high school and college and thinking life was stressful. Now that she was an adult, she could smile at her naïveté. Once Julia started college, she'd have classes and papers and tests. But the real work would begin after graduation as she began to support herself with a career and possibly run a household and have a family of her own. "Each phase of life has its own challenges," Cheryl said. "Even though you'll have a lot of your time scheduled for you over these next four years, remember to take time to soak it in. Enjoy it."

A shadow crossed Julia's face. "I'm sure I will."

# Chapter Six

Cheryl woke up early Saturday morning. She'd had trouble falling asleep last night. The excitement of the treasure hunt meeting had turned into curiosity as she wondered why anyone would stage a scavenger hunt in sleepy Sugarcreek. There was no entry fee and she'd seen no sponsor ads, which made her wonder what Lori's boss's incentive might be. Just a love of scavenger hunts? That seemed strange. She'd finally decided that perhaps she should stop worrying so much and just enjoy the adventure. She'd given Julia that advice—to enjoy the present and not worry about the future—yet she found herself doing that very thing at times. She'd finally fallen into a fitful sleep plagued by dreams of running all over town chasing clues and never finding one.

Once she dragged herself out of bed, she flipped through her closet and finally settled on a pair of dark denim capri pants and a turquoise top. She did her hair and makeup and glanced in the mirror one last time. Her short red hair had a tendency to look a little unkempt, but today it was behaving. In the kitchen she was surprised to find Julia pulling a fresh batch of muffins from the oven.

"Wow, it smells great in here. But you didn't have to do that," Cheryl said.

"I didn't mind at all," said Julia. "I love to make these."

"Are you sure you don't want to come with us today? From what Lori said last night, I think it will be a lot of fun."

Julia put a dab of butter on each muffin. "Thanks. I appreciate the invitation," she said. "But I think I'd like to do some sightseeing if that's okay."

"Of course, that's fine with me. I just wanted to make sure you know that you're welcome."

Julia had asked several questions about Levi last night after the treasure hunt meeting. She seemed a bit suspicious about the status of Cheryl and Levi's relationship, but Cheryl had finally convinced her that they were just good friends.

Cheryl bit into a steaming hot blueberry muffin. "These are amazing. And by amazing, I mean better than a bakery," she said. "If I were as good a cook as you, I'd be as big as a house."

Julia giggled. "My mom won't let me make muffins when she's at home. She says no one needs all the carbs, especially her."

Cheryl picked up a muffin from the plate. "Well I'll say this—if you lived in Sugarcreek, we could sell these at the Swiss Miss." She grinned. "And probably sell out each day." She made a mental note to check with Naomi to see if she had a muffin recipe she might like to make for the store. Individually wrapped muffins might be a good seller for tourists and locals alike. Who wouldn't want a quick and delicious treat they could grab and eat on the go?

Julia's face lit up. "That's so sweet," she said. "But I don't know about that. I mean, from the little that I've seen, people around here are used to pretty amazing food. So I'm not sure my muffins would really measure up."

"Trust me, they do." Cheryl scooped up a second muffin. "Definitely."

Once they were through with breakfast, Cheryl and Julia straightened the kitchen. "I really appreciate your helping out," Cheryl said. "You know you don't have to. You're the guest, and I'd be glad to do the cooking and cleaning up."

Julia shrugged. "This is just what I do. Since I was a little girl, the kitchen has always been my favorite room in the house. My mom was always more of a takeout kind of person, you know? There's nothing wrong with that. She's busy and for her, food and cooking don't bring joy. It's just something she has to do to sustain herself. But for me, I love to eat and to cook new things—and also go to those old standby comfort food dishes as well. My dad is more like me, but he's had some issues with his cholesterol and blood sugar, so Mom has him on a pretty bland diet now." She grinned. "I sneak him a few of his favorites every now and then though."

Cheryl emptied her coffee cup in the sink and rinsed it out. "I'm sure he appreciates that." She wiped her hands on a towel. "Are you absolutely sure you don't want to go with us today?" She was supposed to meet Levi soon.

"That's okay. Thanks though." Julia paused. "Can I ask you something?"

"Sure." Cheryl braced herself for more questions about Levi.

"Does Levi come pick you up with a horse and buggy?"

Cheryl was quiet for a moment. She knew how strange it must seem. "Usually if we're going somewhere together, I meet him at the Swiss Miss or I drive out to his family farm."

"Oh. Is he not allowed to come to the house of someone not Amish?" asked Julia. "Or can he not ride in your car?"

Cheryl smiled and shook her head. "Oh no. It's not that. He and Naomi have both been to my house, and they've both ridden in my car, as has Esther. We just usually meet somewhere besides here because I don't have buggy parking."

Julia grinned. "I didn't even think of that, but that makes a lot of sense."

"Yeah, you'll notice as you go around town that a lot of restaurants and stores have a special buggy-parking area with a place to tie up the horses. It was odd at first, but now it just seems normal." Cheryl smiled. "There were a lot of things that I didn't know about when I first moved here." It had been a bit of a culture shock as she'd left the city and moved to sleepy Sugarcreek to live and work among the Amish.

"Like what?"

"Oh, you know . . . stuff like Amish men who are married have beards and those who are single are clean-shaven."

Julia widened her eyes. "That's interesting," she said. "I mean, if all men everywhere did that, the world would be a different place, wouldn't it? You'd never have to wonder who was married or single."

Cheryl nodded. "Yes, I guess it would." She finished loading the dishwasher and closed the door. "So is there anywhere in particular you're going to visit today?"

Julia shrugged. "I'm not totally sure. I may just drive around and stop wherever seems interesting. I'm going to take my camera out today, and I'd like to get some great shots of some of the countryside." She twisted her long red hair into a bun and secured it with a ponytail holder she'd been wearing around her wrist.

"I hope you'll come back later in the fall. When the leaves are at their peak colors just before they fall to the ground, it is really one of the most beautiful places I've ever been."

Julia nodded. "I'll have to do that."

"At the end of September there'll be a fall festival. Lots of arts and crafts and stuff like that. And of course, yummy food." Cheryl grinned. "It's lots of fun."

"Sounds like it. I'll have to see if I can get away from school for a long weekend or something." Once again, when Julia mentioned school, something besides happiness flashed across her face. Something that looked an awful lot like dread.

Shouldn't she be excited to start the adventure that lay ahead of her? So why did she always look like going to college could be equated with going to the dentist for a root canal? "Definitely. You can stay here anytime you'd like."

"Thanks," Julia said. "Fall is actually my favorite season." She grinned. "I am one of those people who takes their pumpkin flavoring way too seriously. I've made pumpkin bread, pumpkin cheesecake, pumpkin pie, pumpkin cookies…and I love the taste of those pumpkin spice lattes."

"That all sounds good to me," said Cheryl. She glanced at the clock. "I'd better run if I'm going to be on time to meet Levi. Hope you have a fun day. Text or call if you need me." She grabbed her bag and keys and hurried out the door.

Levi was already waiting in the parking lot when Cheryl arrived. He helped her into the buggy with a smile on his face. "Are you ready to find the treasure?" he asked once they were settled.

Cheryl nodded. "I'm ready to at least try. For now we have as good of a chance as anyone." She glanced at her watch. "We can start hunting in twenty minutes." She pulled a slip of paper from her bag. "I brought the clue. Do you think you already know where to start, or do you want me to read it again?"

"Please read it again."

Cheryl cleared her throat. "Here goes:

> "Nothing is planted
> in this garden of stone.
> This city is silent
> so you may feel alone.
> High up on a hill
> and shrouded in mystery,
> there you'll find statues
> and some interesting history."

Levi was silent for a moment. "Garden of stone." He looked up at Cheryl. "Any ideas?"

She chewed on her bottom lip for a moment. "Is there a quarry here? Someplace rocky?"

"That makes sense. And yes, there is . . . but there are no statues there."

They sat in silence for a moment. Cheryl silently read the clue again. A garden of stone where there were statues and history. "A cemetery!" she exclaimed finally. "It's got to be a cemetery."

Levi grinned widely. "You're right. But which one?"

They ran through all the cemeteries they could think of that were near Sugarcreek. "Are any of them on a hill though?" Cheryl asked. "I'm going to claim 'newcomer' to town on this one. I've only been to one English funeral since I moved here and that was only because Aunt Mitzi asked me to go in her place."

"I remember hearing about one place…" Levi trailed off. "I believe there is an old cemetery somewhere on the outskirts of town that was lost for a while."

She widened her eyes. "A lost cemetery? How does that even happen?"

He shrugged. "I think it was from a very long time ago. Maybe just a few families. Probably early settlers to these parts." He cleared his throat. "Anyway, eventually the land was sold and the cemetery was kind of forgotten. It's near some farmland, but it was just hilly enough that it was not good for much. Whoever bought the land just let it grow up since there wasn't anyone left to care for it."

"That's sad." Cheryl frowned. The idea of those people being buried and then just forgotten was terrible. "What happened next?"

"Someone new bought the land and rediscovered the cemetery. They cleaned it up and donated that parcel of land back to the city. I've never been there, but I have an idea of where it is located."

She grinned. "Then let's go."

# CHAPTER SEVEN

They arrived at the hill at the edge of town, and Levi tied the horse to a tree. He offered a hand to Cheryl and helped her down from the buggy, and she couldn't help but smile. He was always such a gentleman. It was a sharp contrast to the way Lance had treated her and one of the many reasons she enjoyed spending time with him.

"Thanks."

"You are welcome." Levi nodded. He pointed out a trail. "I think we should follow that path. It should lead us up the hill and to the cemetery."

They walked in silence for a few moments, but not an awkward silence. Cheryl always appreciated that with Levi there was no pressure to fill silences with small talk. As they'd become closer friends, their conversations had moved from the trivial to deeper, more meaningful talks. Finally, Levi spoke. "Is your cousin enjoying her stay in Sugarcreek?"

"She seems to be. I'm still getting to know her, but I get the feeling the time she's spending here is a welcome break. The problem is, I'm not sure exactly what she needed a break from."

"Maybe she is just nervous about leaving home and starting college. Any time there is a big change, there is also a big impact that goes along with it." He paused and waited for her. The trail they were on had grown steeper.

"Maybe that's it. I remember when I left home for college. I was half terrified to be on my own and half elated for the same reason."

Levi nodded. "Those can be tough years."

Cheryl glanced over at him. "Did you ever consider leaving Sugarcreek?"

"No. There was a time when I was just a little younger than Julia and had some friends who were going through rumspringa. As you know, that's a temptation for most Amish young people."

For a brief moment, Cheryl imagined meeting Levi during rumspringa—a no-longer-Amish Levi. Would that have changed things between them? Sometimes she wondered if she'd built Levi up in her mind as the perfect man just because deep down she felt like he was unattainable due to their differences. But then he'd do or say something that made her realize they'd likely have been drawn to one another regardless of the circumstances. "But you never participated in rumspringa, right?" Cheryl and Levi had talked a little in the past about his younger years.

He gave her a tiny smile. "Right. I stayed. No matter how interesting it might have seemed to me to see how the rest of the world lives, I could not do that to my family. They've been through enough as it is. They are very important to me, and the idea of leaving them made me so unhappy I never really considered leaving. One of my best friends ended up leaving the Amish faith and moving to Cleveland. His family still sees him every now and then, but it is not the same."

Even though Naomi had once explained that the Amish practice of shunning family members who left the faith wasn't quite as strict in their district as in some, it still made Cheryl sad. "I can't imagine."

"I know it is considered normal for young people to leave their families and start lives of their own, sometimes thousands of miles away, but that is not how I envision my own life. I want my parents and siblings to be a large part of my life no matter what stage it is in. I think I would feel that way whether I was Amish or not."

"Your family is amazing," Cheryl said. "In fact, I think you guys are probably one of the big reasons I remained in Sugarcreek last year when I struggled." Cheryl had gone through a time not long after moving to Sugarcreek when she'd considered telling Aunt Mitzi she wasn't going to be able to stay. "And look at me now—I don't know if I'll ever leave. I feel more at home and less like an outsider every day." Her friendships with Naomi and Levi had a lot to do with that.

"That is good to know. We certainly do not want you to leave."

They made it to the top of the path, and Cheryl could see headstones in the distance beneath a cluster of trees.

And two people standing near one of the stones.

"Looks like we are not the first team."

As they got closer, Cheryl recognized the couple from last night's kickoff meeting. "Do you know them?" she asked Levi.

He nodded. "Daed has done business with the man. He is James Ladd, a Mennonite. I do not believe I have met his wife. He is a carpenter, and his family lives between Sugarcreek and Charm."

Cheryl had learned a little about the Mennonite faith since arriving in Sugarcreek. In fact, she'd given thought to that as a compromise if someday she and Levi ever did manage to develop their friendship into a relationship. Mennonites and Amish had close ties and at one time had been part of a larger group but had split due to a few differences. She liked to think of Mennonites as being very much like Amish but more moderate. They embraced things like electricity and motorized vehicles, yet still held a deeply rooted faith in God, dressed conservatively, and held traditional views on family. "I noticed them last night. They seemed sweet together."

The woman looked up and saw Levi and Cheryl approaching. Her face broke into a smile. She was petite, although a little taller than Naomi with blonde hair. "Hi! It looks like we just barely beat you to the clue." She held up a small box and handed it to her husband. "No point in us rehiding this now. We just signed our names on the register." She held out a hand in Cheryl's direction. "I'm Grace Ladd." Grace's blue-green eyes reminded Cheryl of the Caribbean Sea.

Cheryl took her hand and shook it.

Grace continued. "This is my husband, James." She put her hand on the arm of the dark-haired man next to her and giggled. "It sounds so weird to say that." Her cheeks turned pink. "He's only been my husband for two weeks."

James smiled down at her.

"I'm Cheryl, and this is Levi," Cheryl said.

"Nice to meet you both," said Grace.

"I believe we met once before," said James to Levi. "My brother and I were the carpenters who helped your dad with a roof repair a few years back."

Levi nodded. "Ja. I remember that. It is nice to see you again."

The two men began to discuss their respective businesses, and Grace looked at Cheryl with a grin. "Why don't we leave them to talk? Let me show you a couple of the statues that are here. They're really quite pretty. It's a shame this is such an out-of-the-way spot." She led Cheryl toward an old stone monument. "I guess this was an old family plot once upon a time. This monument is for what appears to have been the patriarch of the family." The stone was old and beginning to crumble in places, but it was still a nice piece. "Isn't this whole thing fun?" Grace asked.

Cheryl nodded. "Yes. But I'm still kind of shocked at such a big cash prize."

"Us too. James wasn't sure about participating in the first place, but when he figured out he wouldn't have to take off work, he agreed. Plus we really didn't get to have a honeymoon or anything because he's in the middle of a big job right now. This contest kind of makes up for it."

"Congratulations on your recent wedding," she said. "And I know what you mean about the hours of the hunt. I could've managed to sneak away for a little bit during the workday, but I don't think Levi could have. I wanted to join the competition as soon as I saw the flyer. I'm just thankful Levi agreed to do it too." She smiled. "How many teams were ahead of you when you signed the logbook?" she asked.

"Only one," Grace said. She glanced around. "But I'll bet there will be more arriving soon."

"Who was the first team?" Cheryl was curious. She'd felt like they arrived to the location pretty quickly, and there was no trace of anyone here except for the Ladds.

"I think it's that couple from out of state. I think I heard someone last night say he teaches history at a college. I'm not sure where though."

Cheryl remembered seeing them the previous night. "I know which couple you mean, but I didn't get to meet them. Oh well. At least for now we know we're in the top three teams." It seemed odd that the team from out of state would be the first one to arrive at a spot that even lifelong Sugarcreek residents had to think hard about. But maybe they had ties to the area Cheryl wasn't aware of.

Grace chuckled. "That's right. We're in the next round for now. If we can just find clue number two quickly, we'll be in good shape."

"Did you read it yet?" Cheryl asked.

Grace shook her head. "No. We'd just signed the book when you and Levi arrived. James has the envelope in his pocket. It's sealed."

They walked back to where James and Levi stood.

"We'll let you have this now," James said, handing the box to Levi. "There's an old stump next to that statue over there. It's hollow. The box fits right down inside it."

"Thank you," Levi said.

"It was nice to meet you, Cheryl. And good to see you again, Levi. Give my regards to your father."

Grace and James turned to leave, then Grace stopped suddenly. "The two of you should come to the cookout our church is having tomorrow afternoon. It will be fun. We're going to eat and play volleyball."

Cheryl and Levi exchanged glances.

"That does sound fun," Levi said. "Cheryl, are you free tomorrow afternoon?"

Cheryl fought to keep the surprise off her face. "Of course."

Grace beamed. "It starts at four. It's Friendship Mennonite Church. Do you need directions?"

"I know exactly where it is," Levi said. "We will see you then."

Once Grace and James were gone, Levi opened the box and removed a notepad and pencil. "Do you want to log us in?"

Cheryl quickly signed their names and the time they'd arrived. She glanced around. She didn't see the hidden camera anywhere, but she knew it was there. Should she wave? Maybe not. That might be too silly.

Levi reached inside the box and shuffled through a stack of envelopes until he found one with their names on it. "I guess this is the next clue." He handed it to Cheryl. "I'll go put this back in the stump."

She waited till he returned then opened the envelope and pulled out a note card.

"Congratulations. You've solved the first puzzle and located the geocache. As a reward, here is your next clue:

"It's time to play tourist.
Sugarcreek is the place.
Go stand by the fence
with a smile on your face.
You'll have to have patience
so wait for the show.
Hour after hour,
just look at them go.

"You may begin hunting on Monday at five o'clock. Join us Tuesday evening for the second treasure hunter's meeting where we'll reveal the top five teams who will move on to the next portion of the contest."

Cheryl placed the note card back in the envelope. "This one seems a little tougher."

Levi nodded. "Ja. I believe Lori mentioned last night that each clue would be harder than the last one. I had a pretty good idea about this one as soon as she read the clue to us. But the new one...I am not so sure about."

"We have some time. Let's just think about it and maybe one of us will come up with it." She grinned. "And I think Naomi will go with us to find this one, so maybe she'll have an idea."

"She'll love that." Levi nodded.

They walked slowly to where the horse and buggy waited.

"Are you going to bring Julia out to the farm for a visit?" Levi asked.

Cheryl had planned to mention just that to Levi or Naomi. "I would like for her to see it. I told her about the petting zoo already, and I'm pretty sure she'll want to visit before she heads to school." The Millers' farm housed a petting zoo that was very popular during the fall. They also offered authentic buggy rides to visitors. Levi managed things, and from what Cheryl had seen over the past year, his business was growing steadily. He'd even hired extra help for the fall tourist season. "I'll let you know tomorrow which day we'll come out."

They climbed into the buggy. "That sounds good." Levi directed the horse toward the parking lot exit. "About tomorrow's cookout...I hope that is okay with you."

Cheryl glanced over at him and noted the furrowed brows. He was worried about something. "Of course. I think it sounds like fun. Grace and James seem like great people, and it would be nice to have a few more friends around here who are close to my age." She wasn't lacking friends in Sugarcreek, but it seemed like most of the people she knew where in a different stage of life than her.

"Good. I felt bad after I said we would be there and wondered if you really wanted to go or if you just felt like you were on the spot and had to say yes."

Cheryl laughed. "There's no need for you to worry. I'm looking forward to it." And she was. Another afternoon spent with Levi sounded pretty great to her.

"You are welcome to invite your cousin. I know Grace and James would be glad for her to go with us. I know a few people who go to the church they attend, and I do not think any of them would mind an extra person."

"I'll ask her." Cheryl could barely keep the disappointment out of her voice. It wasn't that she minded Julia going with them to the cookout. Not at all. It was more that she liked to think that Levi wanted to spend time with just her.

Or maybe she was being silly. Levi had been the one to say they'd attend the cookout together. His inviting Julia could just be further proof that he was a good guy and wanted her cousin to have a nice time in a town where she knew no one.

She settled back against the back of the buggy and enjoyed the rest of the ride.

# Chapter Eight

Sunday morning at church, the preacher referenced the treasure hunt that was going on in town. "In Matthew 6:21 Jesus said, 'For where your treasure is, there your heart will be also,'" he said. "The things you spend your time on are the things that mean the most to you. Oftentimes we hear people decline invitations for things by declaring themselves 'too busy,' but the reality is that there is just enough time in the day for the things that are important. Is your relationship with the Lord one of the things you spend time on? Do you spend more time worrying or more time praying? This time of year is a time of new beginnings. Our kids are getting ready to start a new school year. Our high school football team has a perfect record right this moment. It may not be the beginning of the year, but it's a fine time to turn over a new leaf." He smiled at the congregation. "Before we pray, I'd like for each of you to consider the things in your life that you treasure the most. If you're being honest, it's likely they aren't 'things' at all, am I right? Let's be sure to get our priorities in order as we start this new school year."

After the final prayer had been said and they'd been dismissed, Cheryl was still pondering his words. She and Julia made their way out to the parking lot where Cheryl's Ford Focus sat. "What did you think about the Silo Church?" Cheryl asked. That wasn't the real name of course, but it was what everyone called it. The church had purchased farmland for the building and had left the already existing big tan silo at the driveway entrance. Cheryl had never heard for sure why they'd left the silo, but it served as a familiar landmark and made directions to the church easy.

"It was charming. And there were a lot more people there than I expected. Sugarcreek seems like such a small town, but that was a fairly large crowd."

Cheryl nodded. "I felt at home there as soon as I stepped foot in the door. I've done the search for a church home more than once, and it's not always easy. But I really feel like I belong here."

"I liked the sermon today," Julia said quietly. "It's one of the things I struggle with sometimes. Fitting it all in. You know?"

"I do."

"There are just so many things I want to do with my life. Sometimes it's hard to know where to start. But it kind of seems like I've been going about it the wrong way. I shove God in where I can fit Him instead of putting Him first and working everything else around that relationship. Does that even make sense?" Julia laughed. "Sometimes I don't think my brain and my mouth are totally connected. I often wish I could write down everything I have to say instead of speaking."

Cheryl grinned. "You made perfect sense on all counts." She glanced over, noting Julia's worried expression. "Are you okay?"

Julia leaned her head against the seat and closed her eyes. "Yes," she said quietly. "I'm just thinking about what you said about searching for a church home. I'm about to have to do that. I've never done that before. My whole life, I've gone to church with my parents. I never really thought about making a choice about where to go." She looked over at Cheryl. "But now I have one."

"You're eighteen now, right?" Cheryl asked.

Julia nodded. "Yep."

"Your whole life right now is really just one big choice. You're about to be on your own for the first time. Suddenly, you get to choose everything. From what to eat for breakfast to what time to go to bed—and everything in between. That's all up to you. You'll choose a major, choose friends, and choose where to spend your Saturday nights—not to mention your Sunday mornings. It's all up to you now."

"That's crazy."

Cheryl chuckled. "It sure feels that way at first. And I promise you, when you get to school, you'll meet people who don't handle that freedom very well. They'll spend more time socializing than anything else. They'll sleep all day and skip class. And it's likely that after that first semester, you won't see a lot of them again." She slowed down as they neared her street. "Adulthood is full of choices." She pulled the car into the drive. "And today, you can choose to go with Levi and me to a cookout or do something else."

Julia chuckled. "Well, please don't be offended, but I don't really want to go to the cookout."

"No? Hanging out with a bunch of people more than a decade older than you isn't your favorite way to spend a Sunday afternoon?" She grinned.

"It's not that. You're really cool. So is Levi." Julia shrugged. "I mean, I still think you guys have kind of a weird relationship, but whatever." She brushed a strand of long red hair from her face. "I kinda just want to take a nap this afternoon. Maybe watch a movie till I fall asleep or something."

"I totally understand. And thanks for declaring me 'cool.' That means a lot." Cheryl knew Levi would get a kick out of it too. "And if you want some company today, Beau is a great napper. It's one of the things he excels at the most." She unlocked the door, and they went inside.

"Oh, I fully planned to see if he was interested. I may have to wake him up from a nap to see if he'll come take a nap with me though." She giggled. "I always wanted to have a pet of my own. A cat or a little dog to keep me company. Mom hates the idea of an animal inside." She widened her eyes. "Pretty soon, I'll be out of the dorm and in my own place. I'll be able to have a pet if I want." The excitement was evident in her voice. "I can choose that." She grinned at Cheryl. "Maybe this whole 'making my own decisions' thing won't be so bad after all." Julia plopped down on the couch, and Beau jumped into her lap. "Maybe I'll get both. A cat and a dog who get along. You know, like the videos people share on Facebook where the dog and cat are best friends and curl up together and sleep? *Ooh*, maybe I'll rescue them from a shelter."

Cheryl laughed at her exuberance. "Slow down there. You still have some time to figure all of that out. But I think that all sounds great, once you're in a place that allows you to have animals." She smiled. "Just remember that there will be a lot of fun choices to make and also some that won't be as easy. Prayer is always the answer."

Julia nodded. "Of course."

After a quick lunch together, Julia went to the guest room, and Cheryl headed down the hallway, trying to figure out what to wear to the cookout. Grace had mentioned volleyball, so Cheryl wanted to look sporty but not too much so. She quickly chose a green polo shirt and dark denim cropped jeans. She'd have plenty of time to relax before it was time to meet Levi.

Once she was ready, she sat down with a new library book but then remembered she hadn't checked her e-mail since Friday. She opened the app on her phone and scrolled through her messages. One from Aunt Mitzi had arrived late last night. She quickly opened it.

Dearest Cheryl,

I hope you're having a good week. I know between having a houseguest and participating in the treasure hunt, you're probably having a busy time. I wanted to thank you for your Skype advice earlier in the week. I went to the team dinner with Ted last night. We had a great time, and I'm so glad I went.

I don't know what the future holds (none of us do, dear), but I'm sure I am where I am supposed to be. Now, whether Ted ends up being a real part of my life or just a friend to spend time with until he goes back to the States remains to be seen.

Either way, I'm glad to have met a new friend. He makes me laugh like no one has in a long time. It's funny, isn't it? How sometimes you miss someone you didn't know existed until they actually came along?

I hope to Skype with you again soon. Maybe later this week? I want to hear all about the treasure hunt and how your life is going in Sugarcreek. I do hope you're settling in there the way I think you are. Sugarcreek is the kind of place that could be a lifelong home if you want it to.

I must go—there's much to do here.

All my love,
Mitzi

Cheryl smiled to herself as she put her phone down. She was glad Aunt Mitzi had agreed to attend the team dinner with Ted. What a wonderful turn of events. And she couldn't help but wonder if Aunt Mitzi had somehow picked up on the stress Cheryl felt about the future. Although she knew that she and Aunt Mitzi would still need to discuss Cheryl's future in Sugarcreek and the Swiss Miss, the closing of the e-mail told her that Mitzi wasn't planning on returning soon and sending Cheryl on her way.

That was a comforting thought.

She got up to go tell Julia she was about to leave but stopped short when she heard Julia's voice through the guest room door.

Julia's *angry* voice.

"It's my decision. Not yours. Not my parents'. *Mine.* Just let me figure this out for myself." Julia paused, likely listening to whoever was on the other end of the line. "I'm beginning to question everything. You aren't helping."

Cheryl decided to just leave Julia a note on the kitchen table. She didn't sound like she wanted to be interrupted.

She quickly scrawled a note, reminding Julia when she'd return and to text or call if she needed anything.

One quick glance in the mirror and Cheryl was ready to go.

She just hoped Julia would reach out if she needed help.

Cheryl said a quick prayer for the girl to have peace then headed out the door. It was nearly time for her to meet Levi.

# CHAPTER NINE

The butterflies in Cheryl's stomach surprised her. She and Levi were nearly to the Friendship Mennonite Church, and she felt like a child about to go to a new school on the first day. "Will you know anyone there besides Grace and James?" she asked.

Levi shrugged. "Maybe. I have never been to anything at this congregation before, so I do not know who may be there."

"I just didn't know. Since you knew James, I thought you may know some of the others too."

"Are you worried about not knowing anyone?" he asked.

She nodded. "It's kind of how I felt when I first moved to Sugarcreek. Going into a situation and feeling all alone isn't my favorite."

"You are not alone though," Levi said. "I am with you." He grinned. "And I get the feeling Grace is the kind of person who will not be a stranger for long. She is very outgoing. I suspect she will help put you at ease quickly." He pulled the buggy into the church parking lot.

"Nice that they have posts for horses," Cheryl said. "I didn't realize many Mennonites drove buggies."

Levi chuckled. "They do not. But as you know, this area has a pretty large Amish community. There are some people who leave the Amish faith, but they do not go far. Sometimes they cling to some elements of their Amish pasts like buggies. I do not know if that is common in other Mennonite churches, but this one in particular seems to have an outreach for people who were once Amish."

Cheryl fought the urge to ask him what he thought about those people. It had crossed her mind more than once that joining the Mennonite church might someday be a happy medium for her and Levi if they ever took their friendship to the next level. It at least had always given her some hope that it was something that could happen, and hearing Levi admit that there were people who left the Amish faith and transitioned to the Mennonite church fanned that hope. "That's interesting."

Grace and James were waiting on them as they climbed out of the buggy. Grace rushed to Cheryl's side. "I'm so glad you could come," she gushed. "Come on back to the fellowship hall, and I'll introduce you to everyone."

Cheryl grinned and let Grace lead her to a door at the side of the building. She glanced behind her. James was admiring one of Levi's horses.

She followed Grace inside the large room. There was a basketball goal on one side, but today there were tables set up on what would've been the court. There were a variety of two-liter drinks lined up in front of ice-filled cups on one table, and another was full of burgers, hot dogs, and all the appropriate condiments.

"We love having these get-togethers," Grace said. "And there's a whole table of dessert over there." She pointed to a loaded table next to the wall. "We really love dessert." She giggled. "Now come on and let me introduce you."

Grace led her to a kitchen area where several women congregated. "Everyone, this is Cheryl. She is playing along on the treasure hunt that James and I are doing."

A tall girl with a long blonde ponytail smiled. "My sister and I are doing that too," she said. "Isn't it fun?" She stuck out her hand. "Oh. My name is Ann." She laughed. "I don't expect you to remember that though. I know how daunting it is to come into a room full of people and try to remember names."

"Nice to meet you," Cheryl said. "And you're right. I need everyone to wear name tags."

"I wish I would've thought of that," Grace squealed. "I would have made that happen."

Ann smiled in Cheryl's direction. "Grace is our resident planner. We like to joke that she's like a camp counselor because she always wants everyone to be happy and involved." She patted Grace's back. "And we love her for it."

Grace beamed. "I come from a large family," she explained. "I'm the oldest of six. So keeping all my siblings entertained and in good moods was kind of my job. When it comes to organizing people for get-togethers, I kind of have a lot of experience."

"It seems so," Cheryl said. "Everything looks great."

"Thanks," Grace said. "Oh, here come James and Levi now. James loves horses, so I'm not surprised he had to admire Levi's."

"I do too. In fact, Levi gave me a horse for my birthday this year." Cheryl grinned. "His name is Ranger. He needed a new home. Levi keeps it on his farm, and he takes care of it. I can go visit Ranger whenever I like though."

"That's so sweet." Grace grinned. "And a very thoughtful gift."

The owner of an animal rescue had offered Ranger to Levi. The horse had been in an abusive situation and had been rescued and rehabbed but still needed a permanent home. Levi had remembered Cheryl mentioning she had always wanted a horse, so he offered to house, feed, and care for Ranger. It had been one of the sweetest gestures anyone had ever done for her. Some girls might want a fancy diamond or expensive handbag—but for Cheryl, the fact that Levi was willing to care for her horse every day meant more than any material thing ever could. "Yes." Cheryl watched as James led Levi through the throng of people, stopping to make introductions. "It was."

Levi, as if sensing her gaze on him, looked up and met her eyes. He nodded in her direction and continued to meet and greet the men who'd come forward to say hello.

A young man whom Cheryl guessed to be in his midthirties stepped to the center of the room and clapped his hands. "Okay, everyone. We're going to eat first, and then we have a volleyball net set up outside." He grinned. "And for those of you who aren't volleyball players, there are several board games just waiting to be played." He gestured toward a table stacked with games. "Let's all make sure we greet our guests, Cheryl Cooper and Levi Miller."

Cheryl felt the heat rise up her face as several heads turned in her direction. She gave a little wave.

Grace leaned over and squeezed her arm. "I'm glad you came today," she whispered.

The man continued, "I'll say a prayer for this food and time of fellowship, and then we'll get started." He bowed his head and led the group in a prayer.

Cheryl fell into the line behind Grace. "The burgers look delicious," she said as she put one on her paper plate. "There's not much better than a really good burger." She loaded hers with swiss cheese, mayonnaise, lettuce, and tomatoes.

"There are baked beans that are really good," Grace said. "And chips and dip." She giggled. "There's a fruit tray too, so you can feel as if you ate some healthy food." She finished filling her plate and walked toward a table where Ann and another girl were already sitting. "Do you mind sitting here with us, or would you rather save a space for Levi next to you?" Grace asked.

Cheryl glanced around. Levi was in a conversation with James and another man. They were just beginning to fill their plates. "I think this is fine. He and James can probably sit at the other end of the table if there are still spots."

Grace nodded. "I'm glad you two could come." She bit into a chip. "You guys are so cute together."

Cheryl almost spit out the bite of burger in her mouth. "What do you mean?"

"It's just not often that you see a couple where one half is Amish and the other isn't. How is that going to work, exactly? You don't strike me as the kind of woman who'd leave behind things like cars and electricity."

Cheryl felt the heat rise up her face. "Levi and I aren't a couple," she whispered once she recovered from the shock. "We're just friends. His mother has been a longtime friend of my aunt, and now she's a great friend of mine. I met him through her." The idea that Grace and probably everyone else in attendance assumed Cheryl and Levi were a couple shocked her. They never interacted the way couples did. They didn't hold hands or anything. He did hold doors open, and he'd offered a hand sometimes as she exited the buggy, but those were just things he'd do for anyone.

"I'm sorry." Grace's eyes were wide. "I guess I just thought when I saw the two of you together that there was something between you."

Cheryl shook her head. "No. I think a relationship between an Englisher and an Amish man would just be too complicated. We enjoy one another's company, and we are great friends, but we aren't involved that way."

"Do you really think it's too complicated if the two of you are compatible?" Grace asked. "We have a couple in our congregation that started out just like the two of you. A woman who grew up Amish and a man who didn't. This was their compromise."

Cheryl didn't want to admit that the thought had crossed her mind. But she was pretty sure it hadn't crossed Levi's. "Levi has a sister who left the Amish faith to marry an Englisher. It caused a lot of sorrow and turmoil for his family. Because of that, I don't think it's something he'd even consider."

"I'm sorry, Cheryl. I hope you can forgive me for jumping to a conclusion. I didn't mean to make you uncomfortable. I truly thought perhaps you and Levi were a couple like the one in our church and might be searching for a church home." She smiled. "But it is good to have a friend too, is it not? Especially one as thoughtful as Levi."

Cheryl nodded. She'd said the same thing to Aunt Mitzi about spending time with Ted. "I moved here exactly a year ago, and it's definitely been a challenge to meet people, but Levi and his family have been so welcoming."

Once they were finished with the meal, people began trickling outside to where the volleyball net was set up.

"Are you going to play?" asked Levi.

Cheryl glanced over at him, suddenly unsure how she should act. Did everyone around them think they were a couple? Or was it just Grace? "I think I may opt for a board game instead. How about you?"

His blue eyes twinkled. "It has been a while since I have played volleyball. I think I will play at least one game."

She grinned. She'd never really seen Levi play a sport.

"Cheryl!" Grace called. "We're about to start a game of Catch Phrase if you want to play."

She nodded. "Be right there." She turned to Levi. "I'll be sure to come see some of your game too."

"Have fun."

After a rousing game of Catch Phrase with Grace, Ann, and some of their friends, Grace came over and linked arms with Cheryl. "Want to go watch the volleyball match?"

Cheryl nodded.

They went outside just as Levi returned a serve. He was naturally athletic and returned the serve with ease.

"Way to go, Levi!" Grace called.

"Hey!" James said from the other side of the court. "You're not supposed to root against me."

She laughed. "You know me. I cheer for both teams."

Grace and Cheryl settled in and watched the volleyball game in companionable silence.

As the game ended and people started to leave, Grace leaned over to Cheryl. "I stand by what I said earlier. You and Levi seem to have a connection that deserves to be considered seriously, despite your different backgrounds. If you ever want to visit our church, let me know. James and I would love to see you, and we'd be glad to introduce you around."

"Thanks." Cheryl grinned as she watched Levi congratulate the other members of his team on their victory. "I'll keep that in mind."

And she *would* keep that in mind. But she'd also keep it to herself. Levi's friendship was too important to her.

So for now, she'd just enjoy the friendship. Just as she'd encouraged Aunt Mitzi to do.

# Chapter Ten

Cheryl headed home that evening with her mind reeling from the events of the day. She'd really enjoyed meeting James and Grace's friends, and it had been a fun day. It was still hard to believe Grace had jumped to such a conclusion about the status of Cheryl and Levi's relationship. She wondered if she should've mentioned the faux pas to Levi but decided it might only make things weird between them. He might be Amish, but he was still a guy—and in Cheryl's experience, guys sometimes got weirded out about relationship stuff. Particularly when said relationship hadn't really been discussed.

More than all of that though, she'd tried to imagine herself fitting in there at the Mennonite church. Grace had mentioned at least one couple who'd gone that route, but Cheryl wondered what kind of compromise that had been for the couple. She tried to picture Levi adapting to a lifestyle that was more modern than the way he lived—or herself adapting to life on a farm. Was that even a possibility? She did enjoy the animals at the Millers' farm. She was certain Levi wouldn't want to give that up. But was it realistic?

There was no point in dwelling on it until she was ready to talk to Levi about their relationship. And she certainly wasn't there yet. Perhaps she never would be. And she still had no idea where Levi's head—or heart—was. So for now, she'd push it to the back of her mind.

She pulled into the driveway at the cottage and was pleased to see that Julia's car was there and the lights in the living room were on. Perhaps she could take Julia out for coffee or ice cream or something. Between work at the Swiss Miss and the scavenger hunt, she definitely needed to step up her hostess game and spend time with her guest. She unlocked the front door and was greeted by Beau, who was only too happy to let her know he'd like a refill in his food bowl. "Julia?" she called.

No answer.

She followed Beau to the kitchen. A smorgasbord of muffins and cookies sat on the counter. Julia must have spent the afternoon baking. Cheryl was pretty sure she'd gained a couple of pounds since Julia had arrived. But she didn't plan to step on the scale to find out. She'd needed to lose about fifteen pounds for a while now. She certainly didn't want to have to up that number. So in this case, perhaps she'd be like an ostrich and stick her head in the sand. And also maybe she'd walk a little more briskly to work the coming mornings.

She poured a scoop of food in Beau's bowl. He let her give him one good scratch under the chin before he turned his focus to his dinner. Spoiled kitty. "I see you missed me a little. Or at least you missed me being here to feed you at the normal time."

Beau ignored her and concentrated on his kibble.

Cheryl could hear the shower running in the bathroom. As she walked down the hallway, another sound mixed in with the water—great sobs.

Julia.

She paused for a moment and listened to the sobs, and her own eyes welled up with tears. She'd never been able to see or hear someone cry without getting a little teary herself. And from the sound of the cries, Julia's heart must be breaking. Might it have to do with the argument Cheryl had overheard earlier? Cheryl paced the hallway for a moment then decided to just wait in the kitchen. She settled into a chair and took a cookie off the platter. She bit into it and was delighted to discover she'd chosen a chocolate walnut cookie.

Cheryl was on her third cookie when Julia appeared in the doorway. Her eyes were red and puffy, but she was no longer crying. "I'm glad you found the cookies. I baked them while you were gone."

"They are amazing," Cheryl said, raising a cookie in Julia's direction. "I haven't gotten to the muffins yet, but I know they will be too."

Julia smiled. "Thanks." She ran water in the teapot and set it on the stove. "I'm going to make some tea. Would you like some?"

Cheryl jumped up. "Oh, I should be the one doing that. You're my guest."

"Don't worry about it." Julia pulled a box of tea from the cupboard. "I've pretty much made myself at home in your kitchen these past few days. I can do it myself."

"I'm glad you're at home here." Cheryl took another bite of a cookie. "Is everything going okay?" She didn't want to outright say she'd heard the crying, but she also wanted to check to make sure

Julia was okay and knew she'd be glad to listen to whatever troubles might be cropping up.

Julia poured water into a teacup. "I'm fine. I guess I'm just a little extra emotional these days. I never expected life to be this stressful at this stage. I thought the summer after my senior year would be all fun and games, but mostly it's just been about embracing all the changes going on in my life." She sat down at the table, gripping her teacup like it was a life preserver. "It's like one day you're a little kid and your parents are telling you what to do, and then the next day—*boom!*—you're expected to know what to do with the rest of your life."

Cheryl smiled. "I felt the same way. That's only natural. The good news is that you *aren't* expected to know what to do with the rest of your life. It's totally okay to figure it out as you go. Look at my aunt Mitzi. This is her cottage, and the Swiss Miss is her shop. She was married for forty years, and after her husband died, she decided to fulfill a lifelong dream of doing mission work. So if she can reinvent herself in her sixties, I think it's safe to say that no matter what stage you're in, the rest of your life isn't necessarily already decided based on a decision you made at eighteen."

Julia sighed heavily. "That makes me feel a little better to know I'm not necessarily locked in to my decisions. But still. It would be the best-case scenario if I already knew what I wanted for my life and could start pursuing it now."

"What you're saying makes complete and total sense. But I'll give you a little advice. Make those life decisions with prayer. You might be surprised by what happens. My whole journey to

Sugarcreek was definitely something I prayed a lot about. It wasn't the easiest decision to make, but now that I'm here, I can see it was the best decision for me. You may find that with a little prayer, those decisions you have to make that seem impossible—are actually not as tough as they seem."

"But what if God leads me somewhere unexpected? Somewhere I've never even considered before?" Julia asked.

"Then that's where taking a leap of faith might be necessary. I have a friend from college who was bound and determined to be a nurse. She had a hospital all picked out where she wanted to work. It's all she talked about when we were in school. It's a children's hospital that's world famous for its cutting-edge treatments. My friend had dreamed of working there since she was a little girl and had a friend who went there for cancer treatments."

"So what happened? Did she ever make it there?"

Cheryl shook her head. "She did some of her hours there as part of a course, but that's as close as she came. She met a guy during her last year of school—he was headed to Paraguay to do mission work. Now she's married to him, and they live in South America. She works as a nurse at a small clinic and even travels sometimes. Her husband will preach, and she'll provide medical care to small villages. She says it's her life's calling." Cheryl smiled. "So you see? Sometimes God has bigger plans for us than we imagine for ourselves."

Julia returned her smile. "I like that. I'll keep that in mind. Maybe the key is to pray more, worry less, and be open to what opportunities arise."

"I think you've got it." Cheryl stood. "Now you go on to bed, and I'll finish cleaning the kitchen."

Julia nodded and headed to the guest room.

Cheryl reached into the top cabinet and found a container for the muffins. She opened it and found a yellow envelope holding a folded piece of purple note paper. She smiled to herself. It could only be one thing. A note from Aunt Mitzi.

She sat down and opened the note.

Dearest Cheryl,

I hope my note finds you well. And the fact that you've opened my favorite cookie tin gives me hope that you're storing some goodies. When I set out to hide notes of encouragement around the house for you, I never struggled with what they should say. Until now. For this note, I'll just give you a little advice if you don't mind. It's easy—so easy—to spend precious hours worrying about things that may or may not happen. I think as women we naturally like to consider all the different ways situations might play out, and we spend more time fretting than we do praying. Remember what it says in Philippians about worrying. "Do not be anxious about anything, but in every situation, by prayer and petition, with thanksgiving, present your requests to God. And the peace of God, which transcends all understanding, will guard your hearts and your minds in Christ Jesus."

That is my prayer for you today, Cheryl. That you'll toss your worries aside and give them over to God. Pray instead of worrying. Always.

Much love,
Aunt Mitzi

Cheryl refolded the note and stuffed it into her pocket. She had a box in her room where she kept all of Aunt Mitzi's notes. Somehow they always helped and always applied to her life. Just as she'd encouraged Julia to prayerfully consider her decisions, Cheryl needed to do the same.

She put the muffins into the container and set it on the kitchen table. She'd take some to work tomorrow—it was usually Naomi or Esther who brought goodies to her. Now she could return the favor. Once she was finished, she found the paper in her purse where she'd written down the next clue. She'd ponder it tonight before she went to sleep.

Tomorrow was a new day in the treasure hunt, and so far it looked like she and Levi were still in the running to make it to the next round.

And Cheryl intended to keep it that way.

# CHAPTER ELEVEN

Monday morning Cheryl awoke to a pleasant surprise. It was the first time since May that she'd reached for the quilt that was folded up at the bottom of her bed. The first hint of fall was finally in the air. She snuggled under the quilt for a moment as Beau inspected it. He gave it his stamp of approval and curled up in the center of it once Cheryl got up to get ready for the day.

She dressed quickly and went to the kitchen. Julia must still be sleeping. She grabbed the container of muffins and put them in her bag then scrawled a note to Julia and left it on the table.

Once she persuaded Beau to leave the cozy quilt, she loaded him in the kitty carrier and they headed to the Swiss Miss. Fall was definitely on the way. The air wasn't cool just yet, but cooler than it had been. The leaves were just beginning to change. Cheryl had always thought some of God's loveliest handiwork was best observed in the fall colors.

She unlocked the Swiss Miss and rushed to the alarm. Her heart always raced a little faster when she heard the slow beeps that sounded until the proper code was entered. Today though, no beeps.

Looked like she'd forgotten to set the alarm on Friday afternoon.

Again.

She laughed to herself and let Beau out of his carrier. A lot of good the alarm system would do if she kept forgetting to arm it. She might have to start setting an alarm on her phone to remind her to set the alarm at the shop... but the idea of setting an alarm *for* an alarm seemed a little nuts.

She walked past the potbellied stove that provided warmth during the cold months. "It won't be long till you're up and running again," she said then glanced around. Thankfully Beau was the only one around to hear her talk to an object, and he wouldn't tell anyone. She quickly finished all the opening-the-store tasks and finally poured herself a cup of coffee. She was never more thankful to have left the banking world than Monday mornings. It used to be that she'd drag herself to work on Mondays with a sense of dread. These days she opened the Swiss Miss on Mondays with the anticipation of seeing friends and talking to tourists about the sights and tastes of Sugarcreek. Being happy at her place of work made all the difference in the rest of her life. She no longer counted down the hours till she was off work and instead embraced the time she spent in the store.

Ten minutes before the store opened, the bell above the door jingled. Kathy Snyder stepped inside.

"Good morning, Cheryl." Kathy strode down the aisle to the counter. "Did you have a good weekend?"

Cheryl filled her in on the happenings of the weekend.

"Wow," Kathy said once Cheryl was finished. "You've had an eventful couple of days."

"It's like Naomi says—when it rains, it pours. So many weekends are spent running errands or relaxing with a good book. Seems like I'm in a busy season right now." Cheryl opened the container of muffins and offered one to Kathy. "Julia made them."

Kathy selected one and took a bite. "Pumpkin," she said. "And it's very good. My customers would go crazy for this over the next couple of months. Sometimes it seems like all I have to do to guarantee a top seller is put the word *pumpkin* in it."

Cheryl laughed. "Maybe I should add some pumpkin-themed goods to the store. And I'll mention your compliment to Julia. I think she'll be pleased to hear it."

"By the way, I can't say that I'm surprised that your new friend Grace assumed you and Levi may be a couple." She looked knowingly at Cheryl. "I happened to see the two of you laughing about something the other night at the treasure hunt meeting. It occurred to me then that you certainly get along well. I can see that someone who didn't know you might think there was more than just friendship brewing."

"Even though he's Amish and I'm not?" Cheryl asked.

Kathy laughed. "Haven't you learned by now that love has no boundaries? Every great love story has certain obstacles, and true love always manages to overcome them."

"Well yeah. But in this case, that would be a pretty big obstacle."

"Maybe." Kathy grinned. "No one else gets to say what obstacle is too big for you. You're the one who has to decide if something is worth the trouble that comes with it. Not just in love, but in all of life. Sometimes I read Mitzi's letters and think to myself there is no way I could deal with what she's dealing with. No way could I stand the spotty electricity and different customs. But she thrives there. What I'd see as an insurmountable obstacle, she sees as her being able to live out her dream."

"So it's all a matter of perspective."

"I believe so." Kathy nodded. "Speaking of Mitzi, any word from her about her new friend?"

Cheryl nodded. "I had an e-mail over the weekend. She ended up attending the team dinner with him, and it sounds like she had a nice time. I'm hopeful I'll get to Skype with her later this week." She grinned. "I want to hear some details."

"Definitely." Kathy plucked another muffin from the container. "One for the road." She smiled. "I guess you'll be out scavenger hunting again this afternoon?"

"That's the plan. Once Levi is done with work, we'll go try to find the location."

"We finally found the first clue yesterday, but we were pretty far down on the list of competitors. We're going to try again on this next clue, but I don't foresee making the final five." Kathy turned to go. "Either way, it's been a fun time."

"You never know," Cheryl said. They said their good-byes, and Kathy headed across the street to the Honey Bee Café.

Cheryl had just settled in with her coffee once more and was making a list of ideas for fall specials when the bell jingled again. This time Ben Vogel stepped inside. He glanced around.

"Rueben isn't here," Cheryl called. "It's just me and Beau for now."

Ben sauntered over to the table that held a checkerboard. "I'll wait. He'll be here." Although Rueben had remained committed to the Amish faith, Ben had distanced himself from the Amish fifty years ago. The brothers met most days at the Swiss Miss for a game of checkers.

"Would you like some coffee?" Cheryl asked. "I just brewed a fresh pot." She liked to keep coffee brewed for both herself and her visitors. When the weather got a little cooler, she'd add hot chocolate to the mix as well.

Ben nodded. "That would be great."

Cheryl poured him a fresh cup, remembering that he liked just a dash of sugar and cream. She handed it to him. "I also have some yummy muffins that my cousin made. They're pumpkin."

Ben patted his belly. "I shouldn't. I'm trying to watch my weight." He smiled. "Besides, I already had eggs and bacon." He sat down at the table in front of the checkerboard and began dividing the checkers—red for him, black for Rueben. "I saw you at that treasure hunt meeting," he said finally.

"I didn't know you were participating. Did you find the first clue already?" She couldn't hide her surprise that Ben was taking part in the hunt.

He harrumphed. "Don't think I'd call it much of a clue. Everybody knows about the so-called lost cemetery."

Cheryl hadn't known about it and Levi hadn't solved it right away, but she didn't mention that. "Even so, there was still the matter of locating the box that contained the next clue. So just knowing the general location wouldn't have been that much help."

"If you can read a compass, you can find the location." Ben took a sip of coffee. "We would've been a lot faster except that Rueben insisted on taking his horse and buggy. His horse is as old as him and just as slow." He laughed. "But I guess I don't have room to talk."

Cheryl hid a smile. So the brothers were taking part together?

"Don't look so surprised. I thought it sounded like a fun thing to do. If we win, he's donating his half of the prize money to the community fund his church oversees. We've been in these parts for a long time—longer than most. So the way I see it, we have as much a chance at winning as the next team." He leaned forward, a gleam in his eye. "At least we would if Rueben had a faster horse."

She grinned. The brothers always appeared gruff toward each other, but the fondness they shared was evident. "Good luck."

"Same to you. Maybe I'll see you tomorrow night."

Cheryl checked the clock. It was time to put the Open sign out. A little later it seemed like as soon as the sign was turned, the shop was full. She barely had a chance to catch her breath between two tour groups, so she was relieved when Esther arrived.

"I am sorry to be late, Cheryl," Esther said. "One of our Nigerian Dwarf goats had twins this morning. I was tending to them and lost track of the time." Esther's love of animals was well known as one of her endearing qualities. She was particularly fond of the small blue-eyed goats, and Cheryl knew she could often be found in their stall. Seth had once joked that the goats loved to be rocked by Esther like babies, and Cheryl suspected there was truth to his joke.

"No worries. I'll have to come see the new little ones sometime soon. I'll bet they're adorable."

Esther beamed. "They are. And they weigh about two pounds each. I have not chosen names yet though." She grinned. "I need to wait and get to know their personalities first."

"Makes sense." Cheryl smiled. "I talked to Levi about bringing my cousin out to the farm on Friday afternoon. This is just one more reason to visit."

"Ja. She will love them." Esther slipped her Swiss Miss apron over her dress. "Now I will get to work."

Cheryl nodded as Esther hurried off to assist a woman with a quilt purchase. Esther was such a joy to work with.

The lunch crowd began to thin out, and Cheryl realized her own stomach was rumbling. A trip to the Honey Bee for a sandwich might be in order. Just as she'd hung her own apron on the hook behind the counter, the door burst open.

Lori Groves rushed inside, her cheeks flushed and her hair disheveled. She frantically glanced around the store.

"Is everything okay?" Cheryl made her way to the girl's side. The two times she'd seen Lori, not a hair had been out of place and she'd been cool and collected, even in front of the crowd on Friday. But now she seemed very young and very unsure. "Can I help with something?"

Lori took a breath. "I think someone is trying to sabotage the treasure hunt." She widened her eyes. "I can't get ahold of my boss to see what I should do, and I don't really know anyone here."

Cheryl steered her toward the office in the back of the store. "Okay. Tell me what happened. I will help if I can."

"It started last week. Someone made an anonymous post on one of the big treasure-hunting Web sites and claimed our event was rigged. I got it removed of course, and I chalked it up to someone trying to start mischief online. But today as I was walking around town, I noticed that someone had taken the flyer I posted initially and replicated it. Except that the time and place of tomorrow night's event have been changed."

Cheryl furrowed her brow. "But you made it clear last week that if you weren't present tomorrow night, your team wouldn't move on in the competition regardless of what place you were in."

"Exactly."

"Any idea who might do something like that?" Cheryl asked. She ran through the list of people she'd seen Friday night, but there were so many there—and so many she didn't know. It would be impossible to track down the guilty party.

Lori shook her head. "No. I have entry forms from each person, but that doesn't really tell me if they're honest or not. I just can't believe someone would stoop so low." She sighed. "And more importantly, it makes me worry about what they might do next. Someone must really want that cash prize to be theirs if they're willing to pull something like that."

"That's true. Maybe you can make an exception for tomorrow? So that if a team shows up at that other location, they can still participate?" Cheryl had an idea. "We can have someone show up at the alternate location and wait. They can direct people to the right place." She knew if she asked around, she'd be able to find someone willing to help out. "A lot of people I know are playing along, but my friend Naomi and her husband, Seth, would probably do that if you'd like." She felt pretty confident that once they learned of the situation, Seth and Naomi would step in. It would only be for an hour or so.

The relief was evident on Lori's face. "Oh, thank you. That's a great idea." Her cheeks turned pink. "I should've thought of that earlier. I'm embarrassed that I had such a reaction."

"There's no need to be embarrassed. You're in a town where you don't know many people, and you're handling this event pretty much alone. I can see how easy it would be to get overwhelmed." She smiled. "I'm glad to help."

Lori pulled one of the flyers from her bag. "Here's the fake flyer. I'm hoping that everyone who is participating will just go to the same place we were before. But these look legit, so I'm worried if someone happened to see one, they'd believe I'd changed the time and location."

The flyer certainly looked authentic right down to the font. Whoever had done this was smart. Possibly ruthless. But maybe not dangerous. Still though, the thousand-dollar cash prize was hefty. People tended to get a little crazy when large amounts of money were involved. "These really look like the real deal."

"Yeah. Whoever did it put a lot of time and effort into it. But the good news is that it looks like they got sidetracked when they were putting them up. They were only in one area, so either they changed their mind or they ran out of flyers. Something." She brightened. "Either way, I'm hoping not many people saw them."

That was good news, but someone was still up to no good. "I think you should let the local police know what happened." Cheryl mentally patted herself on the back. There had been times in the past when she'd sidestepped the police and taken the sleuthing into her own hands. But not this time. "I can go with you if you'd like."

"Do you think it's really necessary to get the police involved?" Lori looked worried again.

"I don't think there's much they can do, but I also think letting them know that there may be someone up to no good is always the best bet." She patted Lori's arm. "There's no need to worry about talking to them. Ask for Chief Twitchell. He'll listen to you and then if anything else happens, he's already in the loop."

"That makes sense." Lori brightened. "And I can go alone. No need for you to come."

Cheryl tried to hide her relief. If she had to go to the chief's office and let him know something was amiss in Sugarcreek *again*—and on top of that, she knew about it... Well, she was sure he'd try to find a reason to lock her up just for the sake of it. He never seemed to believe her when she told him she honest-to-goodness didn't seek out trouble. It just had a strange way of finding her. "Great. Let me know if there's anything else I can do." She waved the flyer in the air. "And I'll get a volunteer or two to show up at this location tomorrow night."

Lori thanked her and left, leaving Cheryl lost in thought.

It seemed like there was another round of trouble brewing in Sugarcreek.

# CHAPTER TWELVE

Naomi walked through the door of the Swiss Miss, a gleam in her eye. "I think I may have an idea about the second clue," she whispered as soon as she was within earshot of Cheryl. "But let us wait till Levi gets here before we discuss it."

Cheryl laughed. "Okay."

"Is there anything I can do to help you close up?" Naomi asked. "It looks like you must have had quite a hectic day. Esther came home earlier and told me there were two buses in this morning."

Cheryl nodded. "I think a lot of people must be having a final hurrah for the summer before school starts back. It has been like a revolving door today. I know you may not want to hear it, but I could really use some more jars of preserves. And I need to talk to Levi about getting some more leather Bible covers soon. I know it's only August, but it's not too soon to start thinking about Christmas stock."

"I have some jars at home and will send them by Esther tomorrow," Naomi said. "And I am glad you mentioned the holiday season. I am planning to make some new products that you might want to sell. We had quite a productive pepper crop in the garden this year, so I am making lots of pepper jelly, both red and green. It is very good with a bit of cream cheese on a cracker."

"Oh, that's so yummy," Cheryl said. "I'd love to have some in stock."

"I also have kind of an unusual flavor that Seth thinks is quite good. It is a strawberry jalapeño. Not too hot, but the combination of sweet and spicy really is delicious."

"Put me down for some of that too. I think customers would love it." One of the things Cheryl loved the most about running the Swiss Miss was discovering what inventory would sell well. In her experience so far, anything made by Naomi had best-seller potential. Customers from out of town loved the idea of buying jam or jelly made by an Amish woman, but Amish or not, Naomi was one of the best cooks around.

Naomi smiled. "I will be making it over the next weeks." She looked around. "Is Julia going with us today?"

Cheryl frowned. "No."

"Is everything okay?" Naomi folded a baby blanket and put it back on the shelf next to the others.

"Honestly, I'm still a little worried about her." Cheryl sighed.

"More than the other day with the scholarship?"

"Yes. She and I have had a lot of good conversations lately, but I get the feeling she's on the verge of making some big decision. I don't know what though."

"She is about to be in college. Maybe she is thinking about what she will study."

"Maybe. I don't know. I just keep telling her to pray about her decisions and that she'll choose the right path. I wish I could help more though."

Naomi shook her head. "Sometimes, many times, prayer is the best advice you can give. My maam used to say, 'Everything changes with one good decision...or one bad one.'" She smiled. "I think that is very true, and I have watched that sentiment play out in the lives of my own children."

"I like that." Cheryl had often thought she should write down some of the Amish sayings she'd heard since she'd moved to Sugarcreek. They would make wonderful wall art.

The bell above the door jingled, and Levi walked inside. "It's nearly time to begin our hunt," he said with a smile.

Cheryl glanced at the clock. They still had about fifteen minutes. "Oh, I'm glad you're both here. I want to tell you what happened earlier today." She filled them in on Lori's visit and the duplicate flyers. "Naomi, I know it is a lot to ask, but do you think you and Seth could go to that other location tomorrow night just in case someone follows the fake flyer and shows up at the wrong place?"

Naomi nodded. "Ja, I think we can do that. I will speak to Seth when we get home, but I think he would be happy to help out. If not, I will see if Esther will go with me to wait there."

"Thank you." Cheryl grinned. "Now do you want to tell us where you think we should start with this clue?"

"Will you read it again?" Naomi asked.

Cheryl took the card out of her purse. "Sure.

"It's time to play tourist.
Sugarcreek is the place.
Go stand by the fence
with a smile on your face.
You'll have to have patience
so wait for the show.
Hour after hour,
just look at them go."

Naomi smiled. "I made a list of all the local tourist attractions today." She pulled a piece of notebook paper from her bag. "See? There is only one touristy place that makes sense to me when you consider the 'hour after hour' show that the clue references. I think it must be the cuckoo clock."

"I think you are exactly right!" Levi exclaimed. He chuckled. "I was thinking more in terms of the 'stand by the fence' part. I wondered if it could be the Farm at Walnut Creek, where so many animals are held in by fences all around the farm. But the 'hour after hour' line does not fit there because there are tours pretty much all the time. The cuckoo clock has to be it."

"Those are both great guesses," Cheryl said. She'd wondered about the Farm at Walnut Creek as well. Although it wasn't right in the heart of Sugarcreek, it wasn't far, and it was inside the boundaries of the map Lori had provided at the kickoff meeting. Cheryl had only visited once since she moved to Sugarcreek, and it had been such a beautiful and quaint place. The owners took in animals of all kinds—there was everything from camels to goats to chickens, and they offered visitors the chance to interact with the animals and even feed them at certain times during the day. But it wasn't a zoo. It was a working farm set up to resemble an Amish homestead, and the animals were all able to free range and graze appropriately. She'd have to mention the farm to Julia. She may want to visit before she left the area. "The clock does make great sense though. That's one of the things Sugarcreek is known for, and I think pretty much every tourist to the area stops by to see it."

The World's Largest Cuckoo Clock resided in the heart of Sugarcreek's downtown Swiss village. It was twenty-four-feet tall and a must-see when people were strolling around the downtown area. Each hour Bavarian figures came out and danced to music played by a little band of figures. The clock and Bavarian figures had been restored a few years back, and it was just another fun and quirky thing Cheryl liked about living in Sugarcreek.

"Let us head to the clock first then and see if it is the spot we're looking for," Levi said. "Then if not, we can always regroup and search elsewhere."

Cheryl promised Beau she'd be back soon. "I've got a call to make before we go home so I'll see you soon." She'd decided to call Michelle today, and she wanted to make sure the conversation was private. She couldn't shake the feeling that something was amiss with Julia and wanted to see if the girl's mother could offer any insight.

She locked up, and they headed down the street toward the cuckoo clock. "It seems odd though," Cheryl said finally. "I mean, how can there be some kind of box hidden there? The wrought-iron gate surrounds the clock. It's not like we can climb over it and search." She paused. "Right?"

"Surely not," Naomi agreed. "But I guess I do not know exactly what to expect."

Levi chuckled. "Tell you what. If climbing over a gate is part of this clue, I will volunteer." He grinned at them.

"Deal," Cheryl said.

They made their way to the gate in front of the clock. "Do you think we have to wait till the clock chimes?" Levi asked.

Cheryl looked around. "I don't see any kind of box or anything."

"I also don't see any of the other teams," said Naomi. "That might be a bad sign."

A man and woman stopped in front of the clock, but Cheryl didn't recognize them. "Excuse me," the man said. "We were asked to give you this." He held out an envelope with Levi and Cheryl's names on the front.

"*Danki*," said Levi. "We appreciate it."

The couple walked off.

Cheryl looked around. "That's so weird. Someone is obviously watching this spot. I guess that should make us feel good though, right? We know our times are really being tracked accurately."

"I think we must be the first ones to find this one," Levi said. "It is only ten after the hour."

"There could have been a team or teams waiting here on the hour though," Naomi pointed out.

Cheryl sighed. "So I guess there's no way to know if we'll be in the top five until tomorrow night at the meeting."

"That is all part of the fun," Levi said. "No one will know if they are moving on until we hear the results."

Cheryl told Levi and Naomi good-bye when they arrived back to the Swiss Miss. "I can't forget Beau, of course," she explained. "I'll see you later." She went inside and knelt down next to Beau's carrier. "Just a few minutes. I need to make a quick phone call, and I don't want any witnesses except you." She reached her finger in, and Beau swiped at it. "And hopefully you won't tell."

Cheryl pulled out her cell phone and found Michelle in her contacts then hit the Call button.

"Hello!" Michelle's perky voice flagged her as a former high school cheerleader.

Cheryl identified herself. "I thought maybe we could chat for a few minutes," she said, settling on to the stool behind the counter.

"Oh yes," Michelle said, "I've been meaning to call and thank you for letting Julia stay with you. I tried to get her to come home this coming weekend so she could spend her last week here, but she declined. She's really enjoying herself."

"That's great to hear. She's no trouble and has actually been so helpful in the kitchen."

Michelle let out a tinkling laugh. "That doesn't surprise me. She wastes more time baking than any girl her age should. Jared and I are always after her to get out and enjoy her social life more. Besides that, we can't eat those things she bakes, and most of her recipes are decidedly not low carb. But you know how hard it is to reason with her."

Actually, Cheryl thought Julia might be the most reasonable eighteen-year-old girl she'd ever known, including herself, but she didn't say that to Michelle. "Well I have no such dietary constraints, so I welcome her cooking." She cleared her throat. "Actually, I kind of wanted to talk to you about Julia. I'm a little worried about her. Have you talked to her lately and asked her how she's dealing with the idea of transitioning to college?"

"I spoke to her last night. I think she said you were gone to a cookout or something. Anyway, she seemed fine to me. Of course, she tried to tell me about some silly fight she'd had with Trevor, but I wouldn't listen. She complains about him all the time—I think trying to get me to validate her side when they have issues."

"Well don't you think maybe she may have some valid concerns?" Cheryl asked.

"Oh, Trevor is a doll. His parents are our best friends, and he and Julia have grown up together. They were boyfriend and girlfriend in the sixth grade and have been together ever since. I just don't want her to throw away something so special over some silly tiff. You know how teenagers are."

Cheryl wasn't that well-versed in teenagers, but she did know something about being unhappy in a relationship. "But what if there are things you aren't aware of? What if she is genuinely unhappy? I'm of the school of thought that says if someone has a concern about the relationship they're in, maybe that's enough to at least explore what that concern is instead of writing it off."

Michelle was quiet for a moment. "I understand your feeling that way. There's no telling what Julia has told you. But I assure you, we only want what's best for our daughter, and Trevor is someone who loves her and looks out for her."

Maybe, but did he make her happy? Cheryl didn't ask the question out loud. "Okay. Well, I'm sure you know best. I just wanted to be sure you knew she was struggling a little."

"Julia is always struggling with something. But in this case, she has no need to worry."

"What about school? Is everything going okay there?" Maybe Michelle already knew about the declined scholarship or could shed light on that situation.

"She's in for the time of her life. Truthfully, I'm a little jealous of the adventure she's about to have. What I wouldn't give to do those days over." Michelle's voice grew wistful. "Oh! Will you please let her know that I was able to change her class schedule? I e-mailed an old professor of mine, and he was able to pull some strings and get Julia in his class even though it was full."

"Sure. Was it a class she was already taking?"

"No. I had to replace her Introduction to Politics class with this one. It's an Oral Communication class. She'll love it. I loved it when I was there, and I learned so much from Dr. Roddick. I know she'll get a lot out of it. Maybe she'll even come out of her shell some."

Cheryl had the feeling this class switch wasn't going to go over very well with Julia. "She seems fine to me."

"And also tell her she never texted me back today. I was at Macy's at the mall, and I found the most adorable comforter set. I went ahead and bought it so she can check that off her list."

"I'll have her text you later." Cheryl was suddenly eager to hang up. She tried to imagine her own mother changing her college schedule without telling her or choosing her dorm bedding. Both of those things were important in an eighteen-year-old's world. Actually, those were important things in any adult's world. "Please keep me posted though. If there's anything I need to know before she leaves, just let me know."

"Thanks again for letting her stay. She begged me to contact you. I'd hoped she'd spend her last couple of weeks with us, but she was so adamant. So thanks for welcoming her."

"It's my pleasure." Cheryl said her good-byes then clicked off the phone. Michelle meant well, but she was the definition of a helicopter parent that Cheryl had read so much about. She hoped Julia and Michelle found a way to keep a close relationship yet set some boundaries at the same time.

Cheryl knelt down and grabbed Beau's carrier. "Let's go home," she said, peering into the carrier. "I'll bet we're both hungry for dinner."

Beau purred in agreement, and they set off toward the cottage.

# CHAPTER THIRTEEN

Tuesday after work Cheryl hurried home to get ready for the second treasure hunt meeting. She opened the door and put Beau's carrier on the ground. He meowed loudly until she opened the latch then he bounded off in the direction of the kitchen.

"Julia?" she called. "Are you almost ready?"

Julia opened the guest room door. "Yep." She grinned. "And so is dinner."

"I thought I smelled something delicious when I opened the door. What's on the menu tonight?"

Julia walked into the kitchen. "Something very simple since I knew we'd be in a hurry. Every now and then I want comfort foods. Tonight I made a cheesy macaroni and cheese with applewood smoked bacon. It's pretty much a whole meal by itself."

"Sounds like it." Cheryl scooped some into a bowl. "And let me guess... this isn't from a mix, is it?"

Julia laughed. "No way! Homemade is the best."

One bite and Cheryl had to agree. "This is amazing."

"Thanks," Julia said. "It's the very first thing I ever made from scratch. And by that I don't really mean that I made the macaroni or anything, but just that I didn't have a recipe and put together the ingredients that I thought would go well."

"They sure do." Cheryl stirred the macaroni around in her bowl. "I may have another bowl of that when we get home."

"I made plenty." Julia grinned. "I thought you might want to take some for lunch tomorrow."

"That sounds like a great plan." Cheryl took another bite. "Have you talked to your mom today?" She'd held off relaying Michelle's messages in hopes that Julia would end up speaking to her and finding out the news directly from her mother.

"Nope. She texted me, but I haven't responded yet."

Cheryl raised an eyebrow. Something was definitely amiss. "I talked to her late yesterday. She mentioned that she'd changed your class schedule. Something about wanting you to take a class with a professor she had when she was in school."

Julia scowled. "I'll bet it was Oral Communication. She's been pushing me to register for that, but I had no desire. The thought of standing up in front of a group—no matter what size—makes me feel sick." She sighed. "I should've known she'd try something like that. I know it's a required course, but I really didn't want to take it first semester of my freshman year. She always does stuff like this—going around me to get things done her way, even if it's not really what I want. Sometimes I don't think she quite understands the concept that I'm eighteen and can make my own decisions."

"If you're unhappy with the change or if you want more details, I suggest you text or call her. She also wanted to be sure you knew she'd bought a bedding set for your dorm." She grinned. "When I was in college, my roommate and I got matching bedding. That was one plaid room." Cheryl shook her head at the memory.

"I hadn't really planned to match my roommate," Julia said. "But I did plan to pick my own stuff out." She sighed. "Oh well. What's done is done. Maybe I can pick my décor out when I get my own apartment." She laughed. "Although I can totally see my mom doing that too. She wants to be so helpful, but sometimes she just goes overboard."

Julia had handled all the news better than Cheryl would have—and better than Cheryl had expected her to. It was likely that she was used to her mother's behavior, so it didn't come as a shock the way it had to Cheryl.

They finished their food and quickly cleaned up the kitchen. Twenty minutes later, they'd parked at the sports field. "Lots of people here tonight," Cheryl observed. "In fact, I think there are more cars than last time."

"Maybe a lot of people are curious about the top five teams."

Cheryl nodded. "I'm sure you're right. I know I am." She grinned. "My fingers are crossed that Levi and I will get to continue. It's been fun so far."

They followed the crowd toward the bleachers. Cheryl waved to Lori, and she and Julia took their seats in the stands. "There are definitely more people here than were present the other night," she observed. "And people are still filing in." She saw Ben and Rueben making their way toward the bleachers.

"I wonder who made the top five," said Julia.

"No telling," said Cheryl. "Levi and I were pretty confident about the first clue, but yesterday things were a little different. There was no way of knowing what place we were in, so the news will be a surprise for everyone." She watched as two young Amish men approached Lori. The taller one looked angry about something, and it was evident by his body language that he was pretty upset. Lori shook her head at him, and it appeared she was trying to calm him down. Cheryl couldn't help but wonder what that was about. If someone was really trying to sabotage the treasure hunt, everyone would have to be considered a suspect.

"Looks like the police are here," said Julia. "I wonder what that's about."

Cheryl turned around and watched Chief Twitchell standing in the back of the crowd. She hoped his presence meant Lori had indeed filled him in on what was going on. She quickly explained to Julia what had happened the day before with the flyers.

"That's crazy. I get that everyone would want a crack at the money, but going to that trouble seems a little over the top."

Cheryl agreed. "It sure does. I can't help but wonder what kind of person would do such a thing."

Levi and Esther climbed the bleachers, and Cheryl waved them over. She introduced Julia and Esther then turned her attention to Levi. "Did Naomi and Seth find the other location easily?" she asked.

He nodded. "Ja. We dropped them off there and then came here. We will go pick them up when this meeting is over."

"I hate that they're having to take time out of their day to do that," Cheryl said. "And I'm sure Naomi would've liked to have been here to see the top five teams be announced."

Levi chuckled. "They stopped for ice cream on the way. When we left, they were sitting on a park bench eating their ice cream cones. They seem to be enjoying themselves, so I would not worry about it. Esther and I will fill them in on the way home."

Cheryl had always admired the steady relationship between Seth and Naomi. They approached things as a team, and their love and admiration for one another was always evident. When you were in their presence, you knew you were in the presence of a great love. It was sweet. "That's good." She leaned closer to Levi. "Do you know those two guys sitting on the first row?"

He frowned. "They are in a different church district than we are, but I think they live somewhere near Walnut Creek. Daed mentioned it the other night at the opening meeting. Their family has a farm, but I think they're the last two around to work it." He looked at her, his blue eyes thoughtful. "Why?"

She shrugged. "I saw them talking to Lori earlier. They seemed pretty unhappy about something. I just wondered..." She trailed off.

Levi frowned. "I noticed Chief Twitchell in the back. I imagine he is keeping an eye out for any suspicious activity," he said. "That means you do not need to worry about it. This time surely you can leave things to the police." He gave her an imploring look. "Right?"

"Of course. I was just curious." She turned her attention back to the crowd. "There's Grace and James sitting next to Kathy

Snyder. I'll have to tell Grace after this is over that I have a jar of Naomi's preserves put back for her." She'd mentioned some of the Swiss Miss top sellers to Grace on Sunday, and Grace had let her know strawberry preserves were her very favorite.

Lori made her way to the podium and grinned at the crowd. She was back to her calm and collected self in a simple denim dress and wedge sandals. Her glossy, dark hair reminded Cheryl of a Pantene commercial. "Thanks so much for coming tonight," she began. "And more importantly, thanks for participating. I've gotten to talk to many of you over the past few days, and it sounds like everyone is having a lot of fun."

"We'd have more fun if there was a cash prize at every stop," a man called.

The crowd chuckled, and Lori shook her head. "That's not how it works," she said. "But I can promise that the last team standing will be happy with their winnings." She cleared her throat. "And speaking of the last team standing, let's go ahead and announce the five teams who are moving on, shall we?"

The crowd cheered and clapped.

"In no particular order, here they are. Teams, if you're called, please come down."

Levi leaned over. "This is it," he whispered.

"Ben and Rueben Vogel."

Cheryl clapped as the men slowly made their way to the front. Ben looked especially pleased.

"James and Grace Ladd." A beaming Grace led James by the hand to the front.

"They are so cute," Julia whispered as the crowd cheered.

"Newlyweds," Cheryl whispered back. Grace was clearly much more comfortable in front of the crowd than James. As she waved to different people in the stands, James held on to her hand and looked sheepish.

"Gary and Lynn Calloway." A distinguished older man who looked to be in his early seventies and a petite woman with short, gray hair made their way to the front. The crowd remained silent.

"Do you know them?" A woman a couple of rows in front of Cheryl whispered loudly to the group around her. "I don't think they're from around here."

A murmuring spread through the crowd. It didn't appear that anyone present knew the couple. Cheryl nudged Julia. "We should clap." She clapped her hands together, and Levi, Esther, and Julia joined in. The rest of the crowd followed suit, although a little less enthusiastically than they had for the first teams.

Visible relief spread across Lynn Calloway's face. She smoothed her hair and then leaned over and whispered something to her husband.

"Samuel and Jacob Stoltz." The Amish brothers from Walnut Creek hurried to the front, looking pleased.

Lori smiled at the crowd. "One spot remains in the competition. Before I announce the final team, I want to thank everyone for participating. You have been such a fun group. And keep in mind that even if you aren't on one of the final teams, the fun doesn't have to end here. I have brochures available that will tell you more about geocaching. It's something fun you can do with your whole family. Granted, there won't be a potential cash prize like in this competition, but you can't put a price tag on family time, now can you?"

The crowd chuckled.

"There will also be two more gatherings, and everyone is invited to attend those. We'll have some door prizes and refreshments. I would like to especially invite each of you to attend the closing ceremony that will be next Thursday night. We'll crown the winning team, and you'll get to hear from the sponsor of the event. Don't miss it."

Julia leaned over. "That sounds fun. I wonder who the mystery man is who's behind this? Seems like he'd want to be present for the whole thing, doesn't it?"

Cheryl had already had the same thought. She made a mental note to try to learn more about the mysterious Mr. Arnold whom Lori worked for. "Sure does."

"Without further ado, the final team who will be competing for the cash prize is Levi Miller and Cheryl Cooper."

Cheryl jumped up and clapped. "I can't believe it!"

She followed Levi down the bleacher steps, and some of the audience members called out their well wishes. "Yay, Cheryl and Levi!" Kathy Snyder exclaimed as they passed by the row she was sitting on.

They took their place next to Samuel and Jacob and faced the crowd.

"Okay, teams. It's time for your next clue. This is the third clue in the hunt, and by solving it, you'll get clue number four. The fifth and final clue will be announced at our next gathering, which will be Monday night."

Levi smiled down at Cheryl. "I cannot believe we made it to the final round," he whispered.

"Me neither." She returned his smile.

"Now for the clue. I'll also give you a paper copy so you'll have it written down." Lori paused and looked at the crowd. "And please don't offer assistance to the teams. Even if you have an idea about where the next clue is hidden, keep it to yourselves!"

"Yes, ma'am," a little boy in the third row said.

The crowd chuckled.

"Thanks." Lori grinned then turned her attention back to the teams. "Okay, everyone listen carefully:

> "There is a place
> that you can go.
> It's filled with stories
> that you may know.
> Do not talk loudly;
> that's too risky.
> Your next clue
> will come from Christie."

Some of the audience members began to whisper among themselves.

"Remember, no help from the audience!" Lori called. "This clue is open at 5:00 p.m. on Thursday. I think I mentioned before that each clue would be a little tougher than the last, so for this one you have all day tomorrow and part of the day Thursday to ponder the clue before you go searching. Happy hunting." She turned back to the crowd. "And I hope to see each of you on Monday night—same time and place." She grinned. "Now, please help yourself to the delicious refreshments."

The crowd headed toward the refreshment table, several of them stopping to congratulate Levi and Cheryl.

"Nice to see you again, Cheryl."

Cheryl turned around.

Chief Twitchell had a small smile on his face. "I see congratulations are in order. But I'm not sure you should be in this contest."

She wrinkled her forehead. "What? Why?"

"You already have too much real-life experience findin' clues." He chuckled like he'd made a great joke.

Cheryl grinned. "Well at least this time it's only for a contest."

"As long as it stays that way, there'll be no trouble." He nodded at her and sauntered toward the refreshment table.

# CHAPTER FOURTEEN

Well that's super cool," Julia said once they'd finished their snacks. "I'm glad you guys made it to the finals."

Esther nodded. "Ja. It makes me wish I'd signed up to play."

"Cheryl! Levi!" Grace came bounding over, James following. "Can you believe it?" She beamed. "This is going to be so much fun. As soon as she called our names, I told James I hoped she called the two of you too."

James smiled at his wife. "I think Grace would've liked it if all the teams had made it through to the next round." He chuckled. "She doesn't like for anyone to feel left out."

Grace beamed back at him. "I just like for people to be happy. No crime there."

Watching the newlyweds interact was like a visual reminder of the old "opposites attract" adage. Cheryl admired Grace's bubbly personality, and she suspected James did too. And she could see James offering Grace a quiet stability that she likely craved. Sometimes when Cheryl found herself in the presence of couples so clearly meant for each other, it made her feel a tad jealous that she hadn't found that for herself yet. But more than anything, the Ladds gave her hope of what could be hers someday, Lord willing. "It should be a fun week."

Cheryl spotted Lori standing to the side, scrolling through her phone with a worried look on her face. She made her way over to where the young woman stood.

"Everything okay?" Cheryl asked quietly.

Lori quickly clicked off her phone and looked up, startled. "What? Oh yes." She smiled. "Everything is fine. And congratulations on making it to the next round."

Cheryl wasn't buying Lori's cheery front. Something was bothering her. She decided to let it go though. Maybe it was personal and not connected in any way to the hunt. "Thanks." She glanced around. "I didn't notice anyone coming too late. Hopefully that means no one showed up at the other location."

"That's what I'm hoping too." Lori sighed. "I guess you noticed the policeman here. I had hoped he wouldn't be in uniform, but no such luck." She chuckled. "Of course, even if he wasn't in uniform I guess most everyone would know who he is anyway."

Cheryl nodded. "True. But I'm glad you filled him in on what transpired with the flyers. Someone was definitely up to no good." She peered at Lori. "Are you sure everything is okay?"

"Fine." Lori still wasn't convincing but clearly wasn't in a confiding mood.

"Okay. Well, if you need help with anything, feel free to stop by the Swiss Miss."

"Thank you." Lori smiled.

Cheryl and Levi agreed to meet Thursday after work to find the third clue.

"That was fun," Julia said as they walked to Cheryl's car. "Seems like a good group of competitors. And your friends that just got married are really sweet too." She sighed. "Do you ever wonder if you'll find a love like that?"

Cheryl pulled out of the parking lot before she answered. "I guess." Maybe she should tell the whole truth. "Okay, yes. I sometimes wonder if love and marriage are in God's plan for me."

"How do you know when you've met the right one?" Julia asked. "I mean, you were engaged once, right? Did you think he was the one?"

Such loaded questions for a Tuesday night. "I did at the time or I wouldn't have accepted his proposal. But in hindsight now, knowing what I know, he definitely wasn't the one. In fact, I thank God that we didn't go through with the wedding." Cheryl slowed the car down as she neared her street. "Looking back, I can see all the little ways we weren't compatible."

"Did you not see them back then?" Julia asked. "I mean, how can you be sure enough to accept a ring from someone and then realize it isn't the right thing?"

Cheryl could understand how that might seem confusing. It had confused her when Lance had broken things off. She'd been angry at the time and had felt misled as she'd wondered why he'd proposed in the first place. "Sometimes I think the signs are there. We just don't always want to see them. Does that make sense?" She pulled the car into the driveway at the cottage and turned off the ignition. "But then I see a couple like Grace and James or Naomi and Seth, and I realize that Lance and I never had that kind of connection. I *wanted* to have it. I *tried* to make it be there." She shook her head. "But it just wasn't."

They got out of the car and walked up the path to the door.

"Do you think you could've been happy though?" Julia asked once they were inside. "I mean, if you'd married him."

Cheryl sank on to the couch. She hadn't been prepared for a heavy conversation tonight, but she had a feeling there were reasons Julia was asking the questions. "I think I would've been happy some of the time. But I don't think I would've been as happy as I could be. And at the end of the day, I'd rather be single than in a marriage that's rocky." She looked over at Julia. "Why?"

The girl rubbed her temples. "I guess I'm just wondering how you know if a relationship is the right one. I mean, ever since Trevor and I started dating, all I've heard is how we make the perfect couple. We were the prom king and queen at our high school, and when the photo was in the newspaper, my mom even said how someday we'd use that picture at our wedding rehearsal dinner." She shook her head. "But I've never dated anyone else except for the time I went to the homecoming dance with Mason Hunt, and that was just as friends."

"I wish I had the answers for you," Cheryl said. "And I know that my advice the whole time you've been here has been to tell you to pray about it..." She trailed off.

Julia grinned. "But that's what you're about to tell me, isn't it?"

Cheryl chuckled. "Yep." She patted the couch, and Beau jumped up next to her. "That and talk to your mom about it."

The grin left Julia's face. "I'm not sure that would be a great idea."

"Why is that?"

"Mom loves Trevor. Like she thinks he hung the moon. She keeps saying how perfect this is going to be—both of us at college and how we'll be in the same sorority and fraternity that she and Daddy were in. She probably secretly already has the wedding planned. Seriously. That wouldn't surprise me at all. She makes sure Trevor is in all our family photos, and it literally already looks like he's in our family."

Cheryl wanted to choose her words wisely. She didn't want to overstep her boundaries. After all, she was only able to hear one side of the story. But if things were as Julia said, it sounded like Michelle might need to back off a little and allow her daughter to make some choices of her own. "But have you tried to talk to her? Does she know that you may have doubts? At least I'm assuming that you do, otherwise why even bring all of this up?"

Julia nodded. "Doubts, yes. I guess I mainly just want to take things a little slower. Trevor is a very nice guy. But so much of the time, I don't feel like he understands me. And we really don't have that much in common. He loves to watch sports and play sports. I am way more into art and theater. And I know that we don't have to have the same exact interests. But sometimes it's more like we're from two different planets."

"But don't you watch sports with him and try to understand it because he likes it? And does he do the same for you—go with you to art galleries or theater performances?"

"That's just the problem. No. He has no interest in going to stuff like that, even when I ask him. I got tickets to see *Les Misérables* last year for my birthday. He complained the entire time and ruined it for me. I'd been wanting to see it on stage since I was in junior high."

Cheryl frowned. Maybe this was a case of two people who just weren't compatible. "Have you talked to him about it?"

"Yes. He knows how much I want us to do stuff together. But mostly he does his thing, I do mine, and then he'll end up wanting to come to the house and watch a movie or something. I just wonder how things will be when we go to college and there are even more opportunities to have separate interests. I don't get how you're supposed to make that work."

"Typically both people in the relationship *want* to make it work, so even with busy schedules they make the effort to find time together. But it sounds as if that isn't the case with you and Trevor." Cheryl sighed. It was way more of a counseling session than she'd planned, but Julia clearly needed help. "Do you love him?" she asked gently.

Tears filled Julia's green eyes. "I tell him I do. I mean, that's just what we say to each other. But I don't think I love him in the way I'm supposed to love someone I want to spend my life with."

Cheryl scooted over and put her hand on Julia's shoulder. "Maybe that's okay. You guys only just graduated from high school. Maybe you don't have to love him in a 'spend your lives together' kind of way."

"Yeah, but ... it seems like we're just wasting each other's time then, doesn't it? I mean, if he isn't the one for me and I'm not the one for him, why stay together and pretend we are? That seems like a crazy thing to do just to make our parents happy."

"So his parents feel the same way yours do?"

"They're best friends with my parents. Have been since we were little. We all go to church together and all of that. So I think his parents just see me as part of their family. None of them ever gives a thought to how compatible we actually are. Only that this makes great sense to them—so why wouldn't it work out?"

"I know this is difficult," Cheryl said. "I really think you need to talk to Trevor. And your mother." She smiled. "And pray about it. Maybe not in that order."

Julia sighed. "I know you're right. I just wish there were a way to handle it without having to have any difficult conversations."

Cheryl chuckled. "Sorry. And just a bit of a warning ... adulthood is full of difficult conversations you don't really want to have. That's just part of it." She grinned. "But adulthood is also about being able to eat ice cream at any time of night, even right before bed." She stood up. "Come on. There's some Rocky Road in the fridge with our names on it."

# Chapter Fifteen

Thursday afternoon the bell on the door at the Swiss Miss dinged, and Levi walked inside. "I am a little early," he said apologetically. "I wrapped things up a few minutes earlier than normal and thought I would come in and see if you had any ideas about the clue location."

Cheryl smiled. "I've been pondering that today. A place full of stories where we shouldn't talk loudly...I'm thinking the library?"

"I believe you could be right," Levi said. "But where would the clue itself be found?"

She shook her head. "That part I'm not certain about." She finished tidying up the shop then scooped up Beau. "I'm going to leave Beau in his carrier while we go to the library. I'll come back and get him before I head home." Cheryl locked the door, and she and Levi stepped out into the bright sunlight. "Do you want to walk or drive?" It was a few blocks to the library, but it wouldn't take them long.

"Let us walk. When the weather turns colder, we will be wishing for a nice day such as this to spend outdoors."

Cheryl nodded. "Very true. It's hard to believe it's already mid-August. The holidays will be here before you know it."

Levi chuckled. "It seems to me that Christmas decorations pop up a lot earlier than they once did. I am not imagining that, am I?"

She grinned. "Nope. In about a month and a half, they'll be out in full force." If she had her way, each holiday would get its own special time, but running the Swiss Miss made her all too aware that crowds of tourists loved to see the store decorated for Christmas beginning in early November. Sure, there'd be some Thanksgiving décor, but Christmas would be the main focus. "Naomi told me she had some special items in mind for holiday sales too. How about you? Do you think you'll have some more of your handmade leather Bible covers to sell?"

It had been a feat getting Levi to share his craft in the first place. Aunt Mitzi had tried to talk him into selling the beautiful covers in the store when she lived in Sugarcreek, but she had no luck. He had preferred to only create them for friends and family. Cheryl had been the one to finally convince him to sell them. But she knew he was busy, particularly during the fall months as the petting zoo and buggy rides were in full swing. He may not have time to make more for the holidays.

"I will have more for you by November," he said. "That should be just in time for the holiday rush to begin."

"Thanks." They walked in silence for a moment.

"How is your cousin? Are you still bringing her to the farm tomorrow afternoon?"

She nodded. "I'm bringing her. Naomi invited us for dinner as well, so you know how much I'm looking forward to that." She sighed. "But honestly, things are a little weird with her."

"In what way?"

"I just get the feeling that she's hiding something. At first I thought maybe it was a boyfriend, but it doesn't seem like that's it. She has a steady guy from back home. He'll be going to Ohio State in the fall with her. They do have some problems, but she's been pretty open about those." It wouldn't surprise Cheryl at all for Julia to decide to end the relationship before college began. And from what she'd heard, it seemed like that may be the best plan for all involved. "But I get the feeling there's something bigger brewing. Something she's worried about."

"Have you asked her?"

It was just like Levi to say that. He would probably handle it that way—by directly asking Julia if there was a problem. But that wasn't really Cheryl's style. "Not outright. I've asked if everything is okay, and I've asked how she feels about going off to school. She always says she's fine and excited. However, each time she talks about college, she gets tense."

"Maybe it is like we talked about before—nerves about starting a new chapter in her life. Change is hard regardless of how young or old you are."

Cheryl shook her head. "I don't know. My gut feeling is that it may be more than that."

Levi paused as they reached the Sugarcreek library and smiled down at her. "One of the things I have learned is that a woman's intuition is pretty accurate. Maam has always known when anything was going on with any of us. She has a way of knowing how we feel about things—sometimes even before we do." He chuckled. "You might have that same talent."

Cheryl grinned. "Maybe."

He held the door open for her at the library. "After you," he said softly.

They walked to the information desk. "Do you have anyone who works here who is named Christie?" Cheryl asked the woman at the desk.

The woman smiled. "We have a Cathy, but not a Christie."

"Thank you," Levi said. He turned to Cheryl. "Any ideas?" he whispered.

Cheryl thought for a moment. "Maybe. But it could be a long shot." She led him away from the desk. "Let's check out the mystery section."

Levi gave her a quizzical look. "Mystery?"

She nodded. "Agatha Christie is known as the Queen of Mystery. I think she wrote more than eighty mystery novels, and they're some of the best known and most beloved of all time." It made perfect sense to hide a clue in the Agatha Christie section of the library.

They made their way to the right section and stopped. "There are so many copies," Levi said. "How will we ever find the right one?"

Cheryl paced in front of the books. *And Then There Were None*, *Murder on the Orient Express*, *The Mousetrap*. She'd read several of Agatha Christie's works, and there were still many more she hadn't read yet. But which one could be the right book to house the clue? She stopped pacing. "I think *Dead Man's Folly* had to do with a murder mystery treasure hunt. Maybe that could be it?"

Levi scanned the shelves. "There are eight copies of that title." He took one off the shelf and flipped through it. "No clue in this one." He took another copy and did the same. "Not in this one either."

"Okay, wait. Maybe I'm overthinking it." She ran her finger along each title. There were at least two copies of each title, and in many cases there were more. Except for one. "*Agatha Christie: An Autobiography*. There's only one copy of this one. This might be it." She took the book from the shelf and eagerly opened it.

Inside was a small card.

Levi picked it up and read it out loud. "'Agatha would approve of your sleuthing skills. Take this book to the checkout desk and you'll be rewarded.'" He grinned. "Good job, Cheryl."

She smiled. "Let's go."

They took the book to the desk, where the same lady they'd spoken to earlier grinned at them. "I see you figured it out." She took the book from Levi and checked to be sure the note was still inside. "I'll put this back for the next team."

"Do you have a clue for us?" Cheryl asked. She couldn't keep the excitement out of her voice. Each clue was more fun than the last, but more than that, there was such a satisfaction with finding the next installment.

"I sure do." She grinned. "I just need your names."

"Levi Miller and Cheryl Cooper," Levi said.

She opened a drawer and pulled out an envelope.

Cheryl peered down to try to see if there were other envelopes inside still, but the woman was too fast.

"Here you go." She handed Cheryl the envelope.

They left the library, and Cheryl stopped as soon as they got out of the doorway. "Should I open it now?"

Levi chuckled. "Let us wait till we get to the store. It seems like it is best if none of the other teams know we have been here. Unless of course they beat us to it."

"I know. I tried to look in that drawer to see if there were other envelopes, but the librarian was too fast."

He grinned. "I noticed. I was kind of afraid you were going to injure your neck."

"Funny." She grinned back.

Cheryl unlocked the door to the Swiss Miss, and they went inside.

Beau meowed his displeasure at being left alone in his carrier.

"Sorry, buddy." Cheryl knelt down and released him. "I leave him out when he's home alone, but there are too many yummy things here for him to get into." She walked over to where Levi waited at the counter and handed him the envelope. "You do the honors this time."

He opened the envelope and removed the card with gusto. "Here goes..." He trailed off as he peered at the page. "Nothing. That is odd."

"What's wrong?" Cheryl asked. She looked over his shoulder.

The card was blank.

# Chapter Sixteen

Levi held out the blank card. "How can that be?" He turned the card over, but the other side was also blank.

He and Cheryl exchanged a puzzled glance.

"Could it be a trick?" Cheryl took the card from his hand and held it up to the light. "Invisible ink or something?"

Levi shook his head. "I don't know. I don't see a trace of anything on there. Do you think this was just an accident?"

"There's only one way to find out." Cheryl grabbed her bag. "Let's head back to the library. Maybe the librarian can check the other cards. If they're all blank, then maybe they're supposed to be." Although that didn't make much sense. A blank card didn't fit the pattern of the other clues. "Maybe this is what Lori meant when she said the clues would get harder as we went further along in the hunt."

"Maybe so." Levi sounded skeptical. "But there is a difference in a harder clue and a totally blank card. Something seems off."

Cheryl agreed. She scooped Beau up and put him back in his carrier. "Extra treats for you when we get home," she promised. Beau refused to look at her; instead he fixed his gaze at something above her head.

Levi chuckled. "I think he may communicate better than any cat I have ever seen."

"I never have to wonder if he is happy with me or mad, that's for sure," Cheryl agreed. She locked the door behind them, and they hurried along the sidewalk toward the library.

"Is that Lori?" Levi asked, spotting someone in front of the building. "She looks upset."

Lori paced the sidewalk in front of the library. She was engaged in what looked to be a tense phone conversation. She glanced up as they approached. "Let me call you later," she said into the phone. "Maybe I'll have something to report."

"Is everything okay?" Cheryl asked.

Lori hit a button on her phone and sighed. "It appears someone is still determined to sabotage the hunt."

Levi held up the blank note card. "We thought something strange was going on when we saw this."

Lori took the blank card and furrowed her brow.

"We even tried holding it up to the light to see if it was some kind of trick with the ink. You know, like one more thing for us to figure out." Cheryl shrugged. "But we didn't see anything at all."

"So yours was totally blank." Lori turned the card over and peered at it as if to be sure.

"Wasn't everyone's?" Cheryl asked.

"Hardly." Lori shook her head. "Someone appears to be playing a game with all of us."

"What do you mean?"

"It seems that none of you had the same clue on this card. One team, the first ones to show up, had more of a warning than a clue. Their card just said 'watch your step' with no other information.

They called me first and were so confused. By the time I got here, two more teams had shown up. One team left and hasn't called me, and you two have a blank card. I already checked the other two cards to see what they say. It's just nonsense. Weird little riddles that have nothing to do with the hunt."

"So there are still teams in play?" Levi asked.

Lori nodded. "One team is in there now. The librarian is going to give them a note to contact me for the next clue since it wasn't supposed to open till tomorrow anyway. I'm going to contact each team this evening and give the real clue to each. I'll call in the order that you received your messed-up clue cards to keep it as fair as possible."

"Have you let the chief know?" Cheryl wasn't sure the police would do anything in this situation. No real crime had been committed, but there was definitely something shady going on.

"I put in a call to him as soon as I got here, but he hasn't called back. I wasn't really sure what to report. I mean, whoever did this had to have gained access to my stuff." She shivered. "It's kind of creepy. I guess maybe they got into my hotel room and switched out the cards. Somehow between yesterday when I created the clues and this afternoon when I took them to the library, they were tampered with."

Cheryl couldn't blame the girl for feeling violated. "I'm sorry you're dealing with this. But maybe that will be helpful as far as the police go. If someone broke into your hotel room, then they may be able to do something. There'd have to be fingerprints, right? Maybe even an image captured on surveillance footage in the hallway."

"Maybe." Lori shrugged. "I'll call the police again if I don't hear back soon. I haven't been back to my hotel since I found out about this, so for all I know there could be things missing." She raked her fingers through her hair. "As soon as the team that's inside the library comes out, I'll do that."

Cheryl decided to press her luck. "Which team is inside now?" she asked. Maybe knowing the order the teams had arrived would somehow help her figure out who was behind the sabotage.

Lori frowned. "I hadn't planned to divulge that information." She sighed. "But at this point, I guess it isn't that important to keep it a secret." She narrowed her eyes. "Unless *you* are the ones trying to throw the other teams off."

Cheryl widened her eyes. "We had nothing to do with it. You have my word." She shook her head. "I'm just trying to help you figure out what's going on, that's all."

"I have heard that you have a special talent for that kind of thing," Lori admitted. "I'm sorry. I shouldn't have said that. I'm just not sure how to proceed. I just got off the phone with Mr. Arnold. He's still tied up there and won't be arriving till early next week. He was pretty adamant that I continue the contest. He said sometimes the cash prize just makes people do crazy things." She sighed. "Maybe he's right."

"It is a lot of money," Cheryl admitted.

"I can tell you this, as long as I have your word you won't tell others."

Cheryl and Levi both nodded.

"That sweet newlywed couple was the first team. The Calloways arrived next, and they're the ones I haven't gotten in touch with.

The two of you arrived next. Ben and Rueben Vogel...Ben and Rueben Vogel are in the library now, and I'm still waiting on the Stoltz brothers to show."

"I still find it hard to believe any of the five teams would do something so low," Levi said. "Do you think maybe another competitor could be angry they did not make it through?"

Lori shrugged. "Anything is possible. Just please let me know if you know of anything or hear anything that might be helpful." She nodded toward the library. "I'm going to go inside now just to be sure the other team wasn't in the library somewhere when I arrived. I don't want to miss them." She paused. "Cheryl, I'll be phoning you tonight with the correct clue."

With a final good-bye, she turned on her heel and went into the library.

"I'll write down the clue tonight when Lori calls," Cheryl said as she and Levi walked back to the Swiss Miss. "We can bring it with us tomorrow night when we come to your house for dinner."

He nodded. "I will see you then."

Cheryl went to retrieve Beau and head home. What an interesting day it had been.

She eagerly anticipated Lori's call and the next clue though. Especially now that she'd learned she and Levi were near the top of the competition. They'd need to solve the next clue and find it as quickly as possible on Saturday.

In spite of the treachery going on with the contest, Cheryl was still excited about it.

And still determined to find out who was behind the trouble.

# CHAPTER SEVENTEEN

It's really nice of the Millers to invite us out for dinner," Julia said the next evening. "I've read a lot of Amish fiction, but I never expected to actually be going to an Amish home to eat."

Cheryl smiled. "Naomi, Seth, and their family are some of the most welcoming people I have ever met. When I moved here, I knew no one. They've helped me settle in and feel like I belong. I've shared many meals at their table with their family and have always been made to feel as if I'm one of them."

"That's cool," Julia said. "It's nice to have the kind of friends who feel like family."

That was exactly what the Millers had become to Cheryl. She'd read somewhere that friends were the family you choose for yourself, and there were none better than Seth, Naomi, and their children. "It is."

"Um. Is there anything I should know? I mean, I don't want to totally offend them when they're being so gracious to have me in their home for dinner."

It was nice that Julia wanted to be a polite guest. The girl was definitely more self-aware than most teenagers. "One thing that kind of surprised me is that they pray silently. It threw me at first because I was used to praying out loud before a family meal.

Pretty much everything else is exactly what you'd expect." She glanced over. "Don't worry. You'll be fine." She slowed the car and turned on to the Millers' road. "You're really in for a treat." She pointed out the window. "That's the corn maze. It's just opening this month and will be open throughout the fall. Lots of families come out and go through it. There's a hayride and a petting zoo as well."

"How fun," Julia exclaimed. "I'll have to come out one day next week and go through it. Maybe you can meet me on your lunch break or something."

"That sounds nice." Cheryl nodded. She slowed the car down as they approached a bridge. "This bridge is one of my favorite things. Have you ever been through a covered bridge before?"

Julia shook her head. "Not that I can remember. I've driven through a tunnel, but nothing like this. It's so cute." She grinned. "I've read about them though in some of the Amish books. These are also known as kissing bridges, right?"

Cheryl chuckled. "That's right."

"I can see why. Something about a covered bridge seems so romantic," Julia said. "I'll bet it's beautiful when it's all covered in snow."

"It is. All the seasons are beautiful here, but I'm partial to winter because I love snow." Cheryl grinned. "Of course, I mostly like looking at it and not actually being out in it."

Julia chuckled. "I don't blame you there. I've been skiing a couple of times, and I always find that I do better with a good book by the fire in the lodge than I do on the slopes."

"That sounds like my kind of vacation." Cheryl parked in front of the big farmhouse. "I always tend to lean more toward snow vacations than beach vacations...although I wouldn't turn either of them down." She turned off the ignition and put the keys in her bag. "Ready?"

"Yes. I just hope they like what I brought."

"I'm sure they will," Cheryl said.

They got out of the car and made their way up to the porch. Naomi stepped outside. "Cheryl, Julia. Come in." She ushered them inside.

Cheryl put her bag beside the couch in the living room, and they followed Naomi into the kitchen. "It smells delicious," she said.

"Danki. It's chicken and dumplings," Naomi said with a wink. She knew that was Cheryl's favorite.

"My mouth is already watering." Cheryl grinned.

"And what do you have there, Julia?" Naomi asked.

Julia set the pie carrier on the counter. "I made dessert earlier today, and I thought I'd bring it. It's a new recipe I wanted to try. Honey pumpkin pie."

"Oh, that sounds delicious," Naomi exclaimed.

Cheryl patted Julia's back. "If the rest of her baking is any indication, it will be."

Julia beamed.

Esther walked into the kitchen, and Cheryl was struck for what must have been the hundredth time by her resemblance to Naomi. "Hi," she said warmly.

Julia and Cheryl greeted her.

"I came to see if I needed to set the table," she said to her mother.

Naomi nodded. "Go see if Elizabeth will come help you."

Elizabeth was a little older than Esther, but they looked almost enough alike that they could be twins.

Twenty minutes later, the whole family was gathered around the table. They said a silent prayer for the food.

"Thank you so much for having us," Cheryl said. "Everything looks wonderful."

"Including this honey pumpkin pie." Seth smiled at Julia. "We like pumpkin, we like honey, and we like pie. Put them together, and we may have a new dessert around here."

Julia beamed. "It was the least I could do."

"Are there any new developments with your treasure hunt?" Seth asked as he passed some potatoes to Caleb, who helped himself and then passed them to Eli.

"He asks like he does not care," Esther teased. "But he tries to solve them right along with the rest of us."

"Actually, yes. Lori called me yesterday evening with the next clue. Here goes:

"We're all onboard
for an interesting ride,
so let's take a trip
that not everyone's tried.
No bags are needed,

at least not anymore.

There are no more tickets

since they closed their doors."

The group was silent for a long moment.

"It must be related to travel somehow. A taxi?" Esther guessed.

"Or a bus," said Caleb.

"It could be a museum," mused Naomi. "Or any place that requires tickets for entry. We will have to think of places that have closed though."

By the end of the meal, no one had come up with anything solid.

Cheryl and Julia helped Naomi, Esther, and Elizabeth clean the table and tidy the kitchen. "This goes so fast with so many people helping," said Julia. "It usually takes me forever to clean up after I've cooked a meal."

Naomi smiled. "Many hands make light work."

"I like that saying," Julia said.

"My maam used to say it to my sisters and me, and I passed it along to my own girls."

"I will have to remember that."

Cheryl grinned. Naomi's bits of wisdom never ceased to amaze her. They were always on point. "Thank you for the delicious dinner," she said.

"I am glad the two of you could join us." She turned to Julia. "And I think I may need to write down your honey pumpkin pie recipe. Seth loves pumpkin pie, so I like to make them for him in the fall when there is plenty of fresh pumpkin."

Julia gave her the recipe with a smile, and they made their way to the living room where Levi and Seth were.

"Would you like to go see Ranger?" asked Levi. "And give Julia a tour?"

Cheryl nodded. "Julia, you're in for a treat."

"Oh, I'll come too and show you the new goats," Esther said.

Cheryl followed them outside, eager to see Ranger. She loved the simplicity of life on the Millers' farm.

Once again she was struck by how much happier she was in Sugarcreek than she'd ever been in Columbus.

# CHAPTER EIGHTEEN

Saturday morning Cheryl woke up earlier than normal. She was thankful for Lydia's willingness to look after the shop for the day. She was eager to get started hunting for the fourth clue. She dressed quickly and left Beau curled up on the bed. "Your breakfast will be waiting when you decide to get up." She patted his head, and he purred contentedly.

Cheryl went to the kitchen and poured some food for Beau into his bowl then started a pot of coffee. She sat down at the table while it brewed, enjoying the quiet house. Julia must still be sleeping. That was fine. She quickly jotted down a note for Julia. They'd meet up later for lunch.

Once the coffee was finished, Cheryl poured a cup and added cream and sugar. She sat at the table with a pen and some paper and jotted down a list of scavenger hunt participants. If the motivation for sabotaging the hunt was simply the cash prize, then it stood to reason that the saboteur was on one of the top-five teams. They were the only ones who would benefit by throwing the other teams off.

But what if the deception had nothing to do with the cash prize? That would mean either Lori or her boss were the targets.

Cheryl was still pondering the situation when she left the house to meet Levi and Naomi. She pulled down the long driveway that led to the Millers' farmhouse.

Naomi was on the porch when Cheryl arrived. She got out of the car and made her way to the porch.

"Guder mariye, Cheryl," Naomi called.

"Good morning," Cheryl replied.

"Would you like a cup of *kaffee*?" Naomi asked, holding up her own cup. "I would be glad to go make you a cup to go."

Cheryl grinned. "Thanks, but I already had some this morning." She stepped up on the porch. "Are you ready to find the next clue?" she asked.

Naomi nodded. "I am. But where is Julia? I thought she was going to go with us."

"She changed her mind. I think she's going to meet me for lunch though. She wants to go to Swiss Country Chalet before she leaves next week."

"That is one of our favorite places to eat out," Naomi said. "She will enjoy it." She grinned. "Tell her to order her dessert first." The desserts at Swiss Country Chalet were made from scratch each day, and it was a local secret to order dessert first—to be sure there was still a slice available. "Of course, she has such a talent for baking she may not even care."

"That honey pumpkin pie was pretty delicious, wasn't it?"

"To be so young and to apparently be self-taught—she is very talented," Naomi agreed. "In fact, I may try to recreate her recipe."

"She'll be pleased to hear it."

"Sorry to keep you waiting," Levi called as he headed up the path to the house. "I had a few chores to finish up this morning."

"No problem," said Cheryl. "Take your time."

He grinned. "Let me just wash up, and I will be ready to go." Levi hurried inside the house.

Five minutes later, he stepped out on the porch. "Are you ready?" The women nodded.

"I can drive today," Cheryl offered. "If that's okay."

"Danki," said Levi. "We can give the horses the day off."

"Speaking of horses, what did Julia think of Ranger?" Naomi asked once they were inside the car.

"Oh, she loved him," Cheryl said. "She loves animals but has never had one of her own. I think she really loved the farm and the idea of having so many animals around to care for."

"I cannot imagine growing up without having animals all around," Levi said. "But then I also cannot imagine having grown up in a city rather than on the farm."

"I think Julia is the type of person who would've adapted well to a rural community. She is very into having farm-fresh foods and such." Cheryl slowed as she drove over the covered bridge. "Do either of you have any ideas about where we should start today?"

Naomi shook her head. "Not yet. Do you have it written down somewhere so I can read it again?"

Cheryl handed her a slip of paper from the console. "Read it out loud if you don't mind."

> "We're all onboard
> for an interesting ride,
> so let's take a trip
> that not everyone's tried.

No bags are needed,
at least not anymore.
There are no more tickets
since they closed their doors."

"What about that historic hotel? You know, the one that closed a few years ago," Levi said. "You wouldn't need bags there because they closed their doors. The building is still there though. I believe they are trying to have it approved for one of those historic markers from the state. The building's owner will renovate the hotel and reopen if that distinction is ever made."

"That is a good guess," said Naomi. "But what about something else? Maybe the bus station? Is there a business there that has closed?"

Cheryl shrugged. "I don't know much about the bus station here. The hotel idea seems plausible though."

"Let us go there first then," said Naomi. She gave Cheryl directions to the old building.

Cheryl pulled into a parking spot in front of the old hotel.

"Wait. Do not get out yet," Levi said. "I had another idea."

Cheryl turned around. "What's that?"

"It is the first line. 'All onboard.' What if that is the big part of the clue? When you take a train ride, the conductor says, 'All aboard.' Maybe the first line is a play on that."

"And not everyone has tried train travel," said Cheryl. "But where would we go?"

"What about that place with the restored historic trains? The Age of Steam Roundhouse is the name, I think. They have steam locomotives and historic cars. It is almost like a historic museum of train travel." Naomi tapped the paper the clue was written on. "However, I do not know if the whole place is accessible to the public. I have never visited."

Cheryl thought for a moment. "I know exactly what you're talking about, Naomi. I believe it is open to the public at certain times but not unless it has been posted." She sighed. "I can't imagine that a clue would be hidden there."

Levi sat up straight in the backseat. "What about the old depot?"

"Oh, that is a great idea," said Naomi. "The old Sugarcreek depot was built in the early 1900s. I remember traveling by train using that very depot. It is not in use now and hasn't been for some time. So the doors are definitely closed."

"Sounds perfect to me." Cheryl buckled her seat belt and turned on the ignition. "And I know exactly where it is."

Ten minutes later, she parallel parked her Ford Focus across the street from the old depot.

"Is not that one of the other teams?" asked Levi. "The people from out of town?"

Cheryl looked across the street, and sure enough there were the Calloways. "Did either of you meet them the other night?"

"I did not," Levi said. "But I recognize them from when their names were called."

They got out of the car and waited to cross the street. "I wonder if they are here on vacation or if they have family in the area," Naomi mused. "Two weeks seems like a long time to stay here just for a scavenger hunt."

Cheryl shrugged. "I haven't heard much about them at all, other than Lori saying she'd had trouble getting in touch with them the other night after the library clue." She grinned. "Maybe we can meet them." Cheryl had marked Ben and Rueben off her list of possible suspects in the treasure hunt sabotage. She was sure Grace and James were also innocent. That left the Stoltz brothers and the Calloways. And she had every intention of finding out more about each of those teams.

As they approached the Calloways, Naomi glanced over at Cheryl. "They look unhappy with each other. Maybe we should not intrude."

Sure enough, the elderly couple was arguing about something. Cheryl couldn't make out the words, but she could tell they weren't kind ones. "Perhaps we should make sure they know we're here," she said.

"Goot idea," Levi agreed.

"Mr. and Mrs. Calloway!" Cheryl called cheerfully. "Looks like we had the same idea the two of you did."

Mr. Calloway looked up with a scowl then relaxed when he saw them. He wore a blue polo shirt and khaki pants. With his wire-rimmed glasses, gray hair, and preppy attire, he looked just like some of the professors Cheryl had known in college. "Good luck to you," he said.

His wife smiled in their direction and smoothed her shoulder-length gray bob. "It's nice to see another team," she said. She leaned close to her husband and said something quietly to him then walked over to where Cheryl, Naomi, and Levi stood. "I don't think we were ever officially introduced. I'm Lynn Calloway, and this is my husband, Gary."

"It's nice to meet both of you," said Cheryl. "I'm Cheryl Cooper, and this is Naomi and Levi Miller."

"Do all of you live in Sugarcreek?" Lynn asked.

They nodded. "I was born here," said Levi. "But Cheryl just moved to town a year ago."

"I have been in Sugarcreek most of my adult life," said Naomi. "What do you think of our town?"

"Oh, we love it," said Lynn. She tucked a strand of silvery hair behind her ear. "Gary has family that came from the area, and we've always wanted to visit. It just worked out this year to do so before his next session of classes begins."

"I thought someone had mentioned he was a professor," said Cheryl.

"That's right," Gary said, walking over and joining his wife. "I'm a professor of history at Eastern Kentucky University. I haven't been to Sugarcreek since I was in my early twenties. It's changed a lot since then."

"I guess this is a fun vacation for the two of you then, right?" asked Cheryl.

A frown flashed across Lynn's face but was quickly replaced with a smile. "Of course. We usually go on a Caribbean cruise each summer, but this year Gary wanted to get back in touch with his roots."

"Well, I'm glad you are enjoying your time here. Have you gotten to know any of the other treasure hunt participants?"

Lynn shook her head. "No. We haven't really met many people."

The professor and his wife didn't seem like the type of people who would intentionally sabotage the hunt just so they could win the money, but Cheryl had learned to never count anything out. "Isn't the cash prize they're offering for the hunt amazing?" she asked. "I just can't believe we're down to five teams."

"Seems odd to me," said Gary. "What's their motivation? I keep feeling like there's going to be a trick to this hunt." He cleared his throat. "But it is a nice prize. We've done a couple of geocaching hunts in the past, and the grand prize was never so big."

"We were surprised by it too," said Naomi.

"Well, it was very nice to meet you all," said Gary. "If you'll excuse me, I need to go make a quick call." He nodded at them and walked off in the direction of the old depot building.

Lynn watched him go, a forlorn expression on her face. "He's trying to make sure everything is ready for his fall classes. I can't tell you how many calls he's put in to the library at the university. They're having trouble getting one of the required textbooks in stock. This will be his last year of teaching before he finally retires, so I think he wants everything to be perfect." She forced a smile. "It was nice to meet you. I hope to see you around." She turned to go.

"Wait," Cheryl said. She pulled a card from her bag. "Here's my card. I manage the Swiss Miss. It's a gift shop right in the heart of town. If you need anything while you're here—stop in. We have delicious homemade bread and jam that Naomi makes." She patted her friend's back. "You won't find anything better."

"Thanks so much," Lynn said with a smile. She tucked the card into her purse. "I will definitely stop by. This trip has felt far too much like work and not enough like a vacation. Souvenirs and homemade baked goods will definitely make me happy." With a wave, she headed across the street where Cheryl had parked.

"Ready to search?" Levi asked.

Cheryl frowned. She didn't see the professor anywhere. He'd hurried off in the opposite direction from where his wife went. He would've had to pass them by on his way to their car. So he was still around somewhere. "Why don't the two of you start? I want to catch up to the professor and ask him where his family is now. He visited here when he was in his twenties—so where are the relatives now?" She could read Levi's expression like a book. He was about to discourage her from being nosy. She hurried off before he could say anything.

# Chapter Nineteen

Cheryl rounded the corner of the old red depot building. Just as she turned the corner, she spotted Gary, pacing the length of the back of the building. He didn't see her, so she quickly jumped out of sight, hugging the side of the wall.

"Why won't you be reasonable?" Gary hissed into the phone. "Once and for all, let's get this thing done."

Cheryl strained to hear.

"I'm playing along with this little charade of a contest. I met the girl today—the one who is supposedly the town sleuth. Good call on having her in the top five. But what about those Mennonites? Do they suspect anything?"

Cheryl's eyes grew wide. He was talking about *her*. And Grace and James. What was going on?

"Okay, okay. Amish. Whatever. Amish or Mennonite. Doesn't matter. What matters is if they're suspicious." Gary stopped pacing. "I am very close to finding it. The money is going to be mine and mine alone. You should have taken me up on my offer a year ago." He started pacing again then stopped abruptly. "I'm going to be a rich man very soon, and not only that, but my name will be the one in the news. You're going to be sorry." He scowled at whatever the person on the other end of the phone said then clicked off the phone without so much as a good-bye.

Cheryl hurried back in the direction in which she'd come. She certainly didn't want Gary to know she'd overheard.

Levi looked up as she approached. "Is everything okay?" he asked. "You look upset."

She shook her head. She'd fill him in later once she'd had time to process everything. "I'm fine. Any luck here?"

He gestured to a barrel next to an old bench. "The box was there. I already signed our names. There's no clue this time though. We'll get it on Monday night at the treasure hunt gathering." He grinned. "We were third on the list this time, but it is hard to know what our total time is at this point. I guess the outcome will probably hinge on the last clue."

Cheryl managed a feeble smile. What could Gary have been talking about on the phone? The thousand-dollar prize in the scavenger hunt was significant, but it wouldn't make him a rich man as he'd said on the phone. Something else must be going on. "I can't wait till Monday to find out what the final clue is."

Naomi walked over to where they stood. "I have been reading the historical marker over there." She gestured toward the depot. "I love reading about the history of Sugarcreek. It is so interesting to me to learn about the past."

"Yes," Cheryl agreed. "It seems like knowing some of Sugarcreek's history would've been helpful in this scavenger hunt as well. I wonder how the Calloways have done so well."

She was still reeling from the conversation she'd overheard. What had he meant when he wondered if the teams in the hunt were suspicious about something? Could it be that Gary was behind the odd things that had happened so far in the hunt? She didn't want to relay her suspicions—or the overheard conversation— just yet to Naomi and Levi. She knew Levi would encourage her to stay out of the situation, and she certainly didn't want to drag Naomi into anything until she had a better idea of what was going on.

"Gary said he had spent time in Sugarcreek as he was growing up," Naomi said. "Perhaps he knows more about the area than we might think."

"And as a history professor, I would imagine he is the kind of person who might learn as much as he can about a place before he visits anyway," said Levi. "So that probably explains it."

Cheryl nodded. "It looks like our work here is done. I'm supposed to meet Julia for lunch. Do the two of you want to come?"

"I have some chores to do on the farm," said Levi. "But thank you for the offer."

"I am afraid it is the same answer from me. Esther and I have some baking to do, and I promised Seth we would go on a walk this afternoon once we are done with our activities of the day." Naomi smiled. "But have fun spending time with your cousin. I suspect she looks up to you a great deal."

Cheryl felt flattered. "Oh, I don't know that she looks up to me, but that's nice of you to say."

They got in the car, and Cheryl pulled out of the parking space. As she drove past the row of cars, she noticed Lynn Calloway sitting in the passenger seat of a white sedan.

Gary was nowhere in sight.

What could the professor be up to?

Cheryl took Levi and Naomi back to their house then drove back into town to meet up with Julia for lunch.

Julia was already waiting in the lobby at Swiss Country Chalet when Cheryl arrived. Swiss Country Chalet served authentic Amish and Swiss food and delicious dessert and was one of Cheryl's favorite local places. Julia had been wanting to try it, so of course Cheryl had been glad to oblige.

"I hope you haven't been waiting too long," Cheryl said. "We spent a little longer than normal finding the clue. It was hidden at the old train depot."

"I never would've guessed that, but it makes sense." Julia had attempted to decipher the clue, but hadn't come up with any concrete suggestions.

An Amish girl who looked to be in her teens came over to where they stood. "Are you ready to be seated, or are you waiting for more people?"

"We're ready," Cheryl said.

The girl smiled. "Right this way," she said. "I'm Miriam, and I'll be your waitress today." She led them to a table by the window. "Can I get you something to drink?"

"Water for me, thanks," said Julia.

Cheryl nodded. "I'll have the same."

"I'll be back in a few minutes to take your orders." Miriam hurried off in the direction of the kitchen.

Julia opened her menu. "Okay, what's good here?" she asked.

"Everything," Cheryl said, laughing. "But I am especially partial to the chicken fried steak and mashed potatoes. Oh, and the bread with apple butter is amazing."

"How about the meat loaf?" Julia asked.

"If you like meat loaf, you'll love it. And remember to order dessert first. They cook it from scratch, and sometimes they run out."

Julia grinned. "Sounds like my kind of place."

Miriam returned with two glasses of water. "Are you ready?" she asked.

"I'll have the chicken fried steak with gravy," Cheryl said. "And I want that with a side of mashed potatoes and some green beans." She was proud of herself for choosing the green beans over one of the more fattening sides. "And can you bring some apple butter for the bread?" So much for healthy.

"Ja." Miriam jotted down the order on her notepad. "And for you?" she asked Julia.

"I hear the meat loaf is good, so let me go with that. I would also like some black-eyed peas and the baby carrots drizzled in a honey glaze."

Miriam quickly wrote down the order. "Is that all?" she asked.

"And a slice of apple pie," Julia said.

Cheryl grinned. "Make that two."

"Very good." Miriam nodded at their choices. "I'll put these orders in right away and bring you some bread while you wait."

"So are you starting to get the lay of the land here?" Cheryl asked. "It's pretty easy to find your way around once you've driven the main roads."

Julia nodded. "I have. I've explored all over Sugarcreek, and I've even ventured out into some of the other little towns nearby. I really like it here."

"Where all have you gone?" Cheryl realized she hadn't been keeping very good tabs on her houseguest.

"I went to Dover and also to Millersburg. Both of them are quaint little towns. I went to Charm this morning and visited the cutest little quilt and fabric store. They had handmade aprons and oven mitts that were all made by Amish women. The oven mitts had these little pockets, and each one had a note card with a handwritten recipe on it." She grinned. "Isn't that the coolest thing?"

"I'll bet you chose your oven mitts based on the recipe included rather than the print."

Julia burst out laughing. "I sure did. Let's just say I've got some new recipes to try out this week."

"You sure have spoiled me. I'm not sure what I'll do without you. My kitchen has certainly enjoyed the workout it's received since you got here. And so have my taste buds."

"Yeah, I don't have that many days left till it's time to move into the dorm." Julia frowned. "My roommate sent me a message on Facebook yesterday asking me all kinds of questions about what I'm bringing. I guess I need to check with Mom and see what all she's already bought."

"I'd say so. Time is definitely running short. Aren't you supposed to meet your parents a week from today?" She was pretty sure that's what Michelle had mentioned on the phone.

"Ugh. Don't mention it. But you're right. Next Saturday morning we're supposed to meet up for breakfast and then drive on to school. I don't start class till that Tuesday, but we can start moving into the dorm next weekend."

Cheryl decided to chalk up the obvious dread to nerves. "Well, I know your mom and dad will be thrilled to see you. Although I'll bet their drive home will be kinda depressing."

Miriam stopped at their table with two steaming plates of food. "Here you go," she said as she put a plate down in front of each of them. "Let me know if you need anything else."

Cheryl said a quick prayer for their food. "Dig in," she said afterward. "I hope you enjoy."

Julia put a fork full of meat loaf in her mouth. "Mmmm."

"Told you." Cheryl grinned. "It's nice to see the resident chef enjoying a meal prepared by someone else."

"It's delicious. Of course, the trouble with someone who likes to cook is that I'm trying to figure out the recipe."

It was nice to see Julia relax. It seemed like as long as the conversation steered away from the upcoming school year, she was fine.

So perhaps for the rest of the day, they'd do just that.

# CHAPTER TWENTY

Monday morning Cheryl headed to work in a chipper mood. She'd had a nice weekend, and tonight was the final treasure hunt meeting before the winner would be announced. Although she'd be sad for it to be over—and more importantly, sad to no longer have an excuse to spend time with Levi—she was looking forward to hearing the final clue.

Once she arrived at the Swiss Miss, she let Beau out of his carrier then slipped her jaunty Swiss Miss apron over her clothes. The first tour bus of the day wasn't scheduled to arrive until ten, and Esther would be in by then to help. Things should be pretty slow and manageable until Esther arrived. She busied herself with the necessary store opening tasks. Once she was done, she flipped over the Open sign. *Bring it on, Monday. Bring it on.*

Cheryl was brewing a pot of coffee when the door jingled.

Rueben Vogel walked inside. "Guder mariye, Cheryl," he called. He went straight to the little table set up with a checkerboard. "I will just wait on Ben to get here. He is slower than molasses sometimes."

She smiled to herself. If Ben had arrived first, he would've said the same exact thing. "Would you like a cup of coffee while you wait?"

Rueben raised a bushy gray eyebrow. "I should not, but I have a hard time turning down a good cup of kaffee." He rose and walked over to the coffeepot. "Are you still enjoying the scavenger hunt?"

Cheryl nodded. "I sure am. I'm ready to hear tonight's clue though." She poured coffee into a mug. "There's sugar and cream here," she said, motioning. "Help yourself."

"Thank you," said Rueben. "Have you sized up any of the other teams?"

Cheryl shrugged. "I guess it depends on what you mean by that. I've become friends with Grace and James Ladd. I already knew you and Ben. I haven't had the chance to say much to the Stoltz brothers..."

"And the out-of-towners?" he asked.

"I just introduced myself to them on Saturday. They seem like a nice couple."

Rueben took a sip of coffee. "I guess. It is hard to tell about outsiders sometimes."

"The man, Gary, says he has family from the area and visited here when he was younger. Do you recognize him, or have you heard anyone else say they knew him back then?" She was still mulling over the phone conversation she'd overheard.

Rueben shook his head. "I do not recognize him, but that does not mean he isn't telling the truth. You have to remember, he would have been coming here and staying with his *Englischer* relatives. Even if we'd seen one another back then, we wouldn't have traveled in the same circles."

True. Maybe questioning the Vogels wouldn't get her anywhere. "Well, either way, he and his wife seem to be doing well in the hunt. I just thought maybe someone from around here might remember him."

"Might. But it'd be hard to know who. Especially since I overheard him say the relatives he stayed with had long passed." Rueben held up his coffee cup. "Thanks for the kaffee." He went back to the checkers table to wait on his brother.

Cheryl looked up as the bell jingled.

Esther hurried inside. "Guder mariye, Cheryl." She smiled. "I hear your team found the clue with ease on Saturday."

"We did."

Esther took her Swiss Miss apron from the rack and put it on. "I'm going to come with Levi to the meeting tonight. I'm interested to hear the last clue." She grinned. "I think it is such fun."

It was a slow Monday, and customers trickled in for the first few hours. Cheryl caught herself yawning and went to pour a second cup of coffee. Just as she was about to take a sip, the phone rang.

"Swiss Miss, how may I help you?" Esther said. She listened as the caller spoke then frowned. "Yes, she is." She held up the phone. "It's for you," she whispered to Cheryl. "And whoever it is sounds kind of upset."

Cheryl took the phone and held it to her ear. "This is Cheryl," she said.

"Oh, thank goodness. This is Lynn. Lynn Calloway from the treasure hunt. We met Saturday."

"Of course. How are you doing, Lynn?"

Lynn sniffled on the other end. "Not good. Something has happened. Something terrible."

"It will be okay, whatever it is," Cheryl said calmly. "Tell me what happened."

Lynn took a deep breath. "Gary is gone," she whispered. "And I don't know where he went."

"Gone?" Cheryl asked. "Do you think maybe he's just out for a walk or exploring or something?"

"Our rental car is still here. But he isn't. He's gone." Lynn's whisper had become a wail. "Can you help me? Please?"

Cheryl didn't trust Gary, but she didn't mention it to Lynn. Especially not now. And he likely hadn't been gone long enough to involve the authorities yet. "What can I do?"

"Come to our hotel. You can look around. Maybe I'm just missing something."

Cheryl glanced around. Things were slow this morning at the store. Esther could easily handle things if she stepped out for a bit. "Okay. I'll come. But there's likely a good explanation."

Lynn gave her the hotel information and hung up, still sounding distraught.

"Esther, I need to run out for a little while. Can you handle things here?" Cheryl asked. She had no idea what to expect at the Calloways' hotel, but she definitely felt like she needed to go check things out.

"Ja. That is not a problem." Esther smiled. "Take your time."

The hotel was within walking distance of the Swiss Miss, so Cheryl didn't have to walk home and get her car. When Cheryl had lived in the city, she'd always wished she could walk more—and now she could.

Lynn was pacing the sidewalk in front of the hotel when Cheryl arrived. She saw Cheryl, and for a moment the tense expression on her wrinkled face lifted. "Thank you for coming," she said. "I don't know anyone here, and I had no one I could call. Then I came across the card you'd given me on Saturday, and I remembered how friendly you'd been."

"Of course," Cheryl said. "Tell me what happened and what I can do to help."

Lynn motioned toward the hotel. "Come inside, and I'll show you our room. Maybe you'll see something out of place that will help you."

For a moment, Cheryl considered calling Chief Twitchell and letting him know a man was missing—but he obviously hadn't been gone long. For all they knew, he was out taking a walk or getting a cup of coffee. "Okay." She followed Lynn inside and past the deserted front desk.

"Our room is just down the hall. We always like a first-floor room if we can get it. As we've gotten older, a first-floor room has been a travel requirement of ours. Gary thinks it makes carrying our luggage in and out easier even though our suitcases are on wheels now." Lynn smiled over her shoulder. "I think it's a habit that dies hard. I remember years ago when we actually had to pick our luggage up and carry it—no wheels. If not for me, he'd probably still be using one of those old-fashioned hard-case suitcases from the 1970s."

Cheryl grinned. She'd figured Gary to be in his seventies, and she guessed Lynn to be in her late sixties. She wondered how long they'd been married. "Do you travel often?"

"As often as we can. We never had children, so any extra money we have always goes to what Gary calls our travel fund. We've been all over the world." Lynn stopped in front of a door. "Here we are. Room one-thirty-three." She inserted her key card and opened the door.

Cheryl hung back for a moment. It had occurred to her that perhaps this was some sort of trap. She couldn't guess what harm Lynn or Gary would want to do to her though, so she followed Lynn inside.

The room was a basic hotel room. A queen-size bed sat in the center. A couch, end table, and coffee table served as a sitting area off to the side. There was a recliner next to a lamp. The large dresser held a TV, and next to that was a mini refrigerator. Art in muted tones decorated the walls. It wasn't a five-star hotel, but it was clean and comfortable.

"The bathroom is through that door," said Lynn, pointing to a closed door. "There's also a closet there." She pointed to a second door. "Gary and I were talking about going for coffee earlier this morning. He went outside to take a phone call—I assume something about his class schedule. But he never came back." She sank into the recliner. "I've tried to call him repeatedly, but his phone just goes to voice mail."

It did sound odd, but Cheryl wasn't too worried yet. "Why don't we get out of here for a bit?" she asked. "Maybe go and get a cup of coffee? You can tell me the whole story, and maybe when we get back, Gary will have returned."

Lynn's eyes filled with tears. She made no move to get up from the recliner. "He hasn't had his vitamins yet today. He was going to take them after we ate breakfast. I should have insisted. I've been making sure that man takes his daily vitamins for forty plus years." She dabbed at her eyes with a Kleenex she had balled in her hand. "We haven't spent a night apart in twenty years, except for once when my mama was sick and I stayed with her in the hospital. Even then, Gary stayed till the nurses said visiting hours were over and kicked him out. He was right back first thing the next morning with coffee and a blueberry muffin, just like I like."

The sweet memory wasn't lost on Cheryl. She adored couples who'd been married for many years and were still a team—still in love. Would she have someone to worry over for forty years? The older she got, the less time she'd have with her mate. If God even had that in store for her. Some days she wondered. And yet she knew she'd be okay even if her path kept her single forever. She'd become more and more at peace with that idea over the past year. Still though, forty years of someone to love, someone to travel with, and someone to share a life with sounded pretty wonderful. But only if it was the right someone. "I'm sure you'll be able to fuss over him and give him his vitamins soon. And he's only been gone a short time. I'm sure he'll be back tonight. He wouldn't miss the final treasure hunt clue, right? In the meantime, how about that coffee?"

Lynn shook her head. "Not now. I want to stay here for a bit in case he comes back soon."

Cheryl nodded. "I understand." She sat down at a table in the sitting area near the recliner. It was littered with books and papers. "Did Gary have any kind of health issues that we should be concerned about?" She knew that with people over a certain age, a Silver Alert could be issued. Should that happen in this case?

"Not anything major. He had heart surgery several years ago but recovered nicely. He's still very active and exercises regularly. We've both slowed down some over the past few years, but I guess that's to be expected." She smiled at Cheryl. "Growing old isn't for the faint of heart, my dear."

Cheryl was only thirty-one, and she already believed that. "Do you want to tell me exactly what happened today? And where you think Gary might be?"

Lynn took a deep breath. "He's acted a little strange ever since we arrived in Sugarcreek."

"How so?" Maybe he acted weird because he was up to no good, trying to sabotage the hunt for the other contestants? Cheryl couldn't help but be suspicious.

"He's been very secretive. He and I...We don't keep secrets. We tell each other everything. The good, the bad, and the ugly. It's something we promised very early on in our marriage. But ever since we got to Sugarcreek, he's been like a different person. He gets these calls and takes them in private. I'm not stupid. I know that looks bad. But when I ask, he just dismisses me by saying they're just about work and nothing to worry about." She teared up again. "But I worry anyway."

"That's understandable. But his calls could very well be work related. Maybe he just didn't want to interrupt your vacation by you having to hear about his work."

Lynn scowled. "That's just it. This whole 'vacation' was Gary's idea. I was completely on board with an all-inclusive in Cancun. We'd already talked about it, and I was just about to book our flight when he came up with this whole Amish country visit. I gave in because he was so excited. He promised me this quiet, lovely time together. We were supposed to take walks and explore the countryside. Not to mention that his family roots are in the area. I thought it all sounded great. The main thing I want out of a vacation is just to spend time with Gary and relax before the school year starts up." She smiled. "I know we've told you he's a professor. And he is one of those overachieving types who has contributed to textbooks and had papers published. But I teach too. Not full-time like him, but I do a couple of classes a year in the family and consumer science department. I'm adding an online class this year too. People always look at couples like us and assume that we have plenty of time together since we don't have children. But we both have busy careers. So our travel time is when we really reconnect." She sighed. "But not this year."

"I'm so sorry," Cheryl said. "I'm sure there is a reasonable explanation."

Lynn shook her head. "There's only one thing that makes sense. I think Gary is in trouble."

# CHAPTER TWENTY-ONE

W hat kind of trouble?" Cheryl asked.

"That's what I'm not sure about. But the secretive calls, the way he's been on edge ever since we arrived...It's the only thing that makes sense. He's been popping antacid like it's candy and not sleeping well. In fact, that's what happened this morning. He woke up way earlier than normal and told me he was going outside to take a call. He never came back."

"So what do you think could be the problem?"

Lynn raked her fingers through her gray hair. "That's just it. I have no clue. In some ways, it seems like he's been really worried about something. Always looking over his shoulder, easily startled...The other day I came out of the bathroom, and he was napping right here. I accidentally slammed the door, and the way he jumped, you'd have thought I fired a weapon."

"And he's not like that at home?"

"No. Not at all. He's typically the most laid-back, easygoing guy you could hope to meet. Even his behavior while we were hunting the clues has been odd. It's been like he already knew where things were going to be. He never consulted me on any of the clues or anything. And that was part of the whole 'togetherness' thing that he said we'd be doing—solving them together. But instead, he's had his nose in this old volume of Sugarcreek history he checked out of the library. I guess that helped him find where the clues were hidden. He's been reading it like it had the answers to life though."

Cheryl picked up an old book from the table. "Is this it?"

Lynn nodded. "Yes. I know Gary isn't a Sugarcreek resident, but the head librarian offered him a temporary library card so he could research the history of Sugarcreek while he's in town. He's working on a paper for a scholarly journal, and the local library here has been wonderful to help him with his research. The book is actually due back tomorrow. We'd planned to walk there today and return it."

"I'll be glad to do that for you. One less thing for you to worry about." Cheryl smiled. "I have a stack of my own that needs to be returned anyway."

"Thank you so much." Lynn rubbed her temples. "I just wish he'd call me and tell me what's going on."

"Do you want to call the police?" Cheryl asked. "I know the chief, and I'd be glad to make that call." She could just imagine Chief Twitchell's reaction if she had to call in a missing person. They'd first met the very month Cheryl had moved to Sugarcreek. Over the months, they'd become well acquainted as Cheryl had developed a knack for solving local crimes.

Lynn shook her head. "Absolutely not. If Gary just went for a walk and lost track of time at a bookstore or museum and he returns to find out the police are looking for him, he'd be furious with me."

"Are those things that might normally happen?"

"On a regular Saturday at home, yes. He might pop into a flea market or a used bookstore and stay for hours. But when we're traveling together and he's supposed to be right back, it would be highly unusual."

"But it could happen."

Lynn's eyes filled with tears again. "I'm clinging to that hope."

"Do you want me to stay with you awhile longer?" Cheryl needed to run home and also needed to get back to the store. But she hated to leave Lynn alone.

"I know you have things to do. Go on. I may take a shower and walk around the area just to see if I bump into him or if any of the storekeepers happened to see him this morning."

Cheryl stood up and tucked the historical book into her bag. "Please call me later if there are any new developments. And in the meantime, I'll return the book for you."

Lynn promised to call later in the afternoon. If Gary hadn't shown up by then, Cheryl planned to insist that she contact the police. There'd already been odd things going on with the treasure hunt. A missing man couldn't be ignored even if the circumstances surrounding his disappearance were unknown.

Cheryl walked to her house. She needed to put a load of laundry in the washer. It had been piling up over the past few days. She quickly gathered a load of towels and washcloths and put them into the washing machine. She wondered if Julia had any in her room on the hook behind the door. She paused at the closed door and debated about going inside. Julia's car wasn't in the driveway, so she'd never know.

Cheryl gingerly opened the door and stepped inside. The bed was made and all Julia's clothing and other things were neatly folded and stacked by her suitcases. Cheryl took the towels from the hook and turned to go, but her gaze landed on some paperwork sitting out on the desk. She stepped closer to get a better look.

It was a US passport application.

With Julia's name on it.

Cheryl backed out of the room and closed the door. She'd let some of the other things go over the past several days, but there was no way she could do the same with this. Declining a scholarship was one thing, but planning to leave the country was another.

Yes, they'd definitely have to have a conversation about it tonight after the treasure hunt meeting.

She finished loading the washer and headed out the door and back to the Swiss Miss.

Two hours later, Naomi strolled in carrying a basket of bread. "You look tired, Cheryl. Are you not sleeping well?" she asked once she'd made her way to the counter.

The store was all but empty, so Cheryl motioned toward the back room. Esther could handle the customers. "You're not going to believe what happened!" She explained about Lynn's call, Gary's disappearance, and Julia's passport application.

Naomi's eyes grew wider with each point. "That is a lot of things that are unexplained. I have learned though that sometimes there are simple explanations for what seem to be the most complicated problems. Maybe that is the case here." She smiled. "I have also learned that sometimes you have to break down your problems into manageable chunks. It is exactly the same way I taught my children to do the chores they do not especially enjoy. Just a small step at a time and soon you are all done."

Once again, Cheryl pondered the possibility of penning a *Wisdom from Naomi* book. "Well, I suppose if I were to look at these things that way, then I'd first reach out to Lynn to be sure she's doing okay. I get the feeling she's in great need of a friend right now. Then I'd make sure Gary had returned, and if not, I'd convince her that it's time to call for help. And finally, I think I should sit Julia down and admit to her what I've learned over the past week and get to the bottom of the declined scholarship and the passport application once and for all."

"It seems to me that you now have a plan. Put that in action, and by the time you go to bed tonight, you should sleep well."

"Let's hope so."

Naomi smiled. "Seth and I will not be at the treasure hunt meeting tonight, but we will be interested in hearing the next clue. Even though Seth is not participating in the hunt, he still enjoys listening to the clues and trying to figure them out. Levi will be there though, and it is possible Esther will go with him."

Cheryl and Naomi walked to the counter where Esther had just finished up with a customer.

The phone rang.

"I will get it," Esther said. A moment later, she motioned to Cheryl. "It is for you. I think it is the same woman as this morning."

"Lynn?" Cheryl said, taking the phone. "Did Gary come back?"

A sob came through the line. "No. And now I don't think he is going to." Lynn broke off, crying.

"What happened?"

"I went for a walk like I told you I was going to. I stopped in at all the stores and shops within an easy walking distance of our hotel. No one had seen Gary. Then, when I got back to our hotel room, the door was cracked. I thought Gary must be back, but when I went inside, it had been totally ransacked. All the furniture had been tossed, and our things were strewn everywhere."

Cheryl furrowed her brow. That certainly didn't sound good. "Did you call the police?"

"Yes. They should be here any minute." Lynn took a breath. "Can you come here too? I can't even think straight. You're the only person I know well enough to ask to come be here with me."

"Of course," Cheryl said. "I'll be right there." She hung up and told Naomi what had happened.

Naomi frowned. "I will pray everything is okay and Gary is found soon. I will stay here and help Esther close the store. You go be with Lynn. How scared she must be to not know the whereabouts of her husband and now to face a break-in."

Cheryl agreed. "Thank you for helping out here. I'll be sure and let Levi know the details tonight so he can share them with you." She knew Naomi would be worried about Lynn and Gary even though she didn't know them very well. "Please put Beau in his carrier when you leave. I'll come back by and get him before I go home."

She hurried out the door and toward the hotel, her mind reeling. Why would anyone ransack the Calloways' hotel room? Could it have to do with the phone call she'd overheard? Gary had seemed almost as if he were taunting someone. But whom had he been speaking to?

Cheryl rounded the corner toward the hotel and walked through the revolving door. She passed the front desk, nodding at a very worried-looking girl. Undoubtedly, everyone at the hotel was on high alert over Gary's disappearance and the break-in. She slowed down as she approached the room.

"Hold it right there," a voice from behind her said.

She turned slowly. "Hi, Chief." She managed a feeble smile. "How are you?"

Chief Twitchell raised one eyebrow in her direction. "I'd like to say that I'm surprised to see you here, Cheryl." He shook his head. "But frankly it doesn't surprise me one bit. Do you want to explain how you're connected to this case, or should I guess?"

She nodded. "I met Lynn and Gary while participating in the treasure hunt. Lynn and I hit it off, so this morning when Gary didn't come back to the hotel when he was supposed to, she called me."

"And you didn't consider callin' me?" Chief Twitchell interrupted her. "Did you not think that might be an important thing to let us know? Or did you go lookin' for him yourself?"

Cheryl bristled. "I urged her to call you, but she was adamant that she didn't want to yet. She thought perhaps he'd just lost track of time and was at a bookstore or museum or something. I didn't want to raise a false alarm, and I really thought it was Lynn's decision as to when to contact you."

"That's the problem I'm havin' with this little scenario. Lynn has a missing husband and no alibi for the time frame when he went missing. Did it ever occur to you that maybe she had somethin' to do with this?" The chief peered at her.

She shook her head. Lynn was a grandmotherly woman who, as Cheryl's momma would say, was no bigger than a minute. The idea that she had something to do with her husband's disappearance seemed absurd. "Absolutely not. She was so upset this morning when I got here, and when she called to tell me their room had been broken into, she was crying. I think I'm a pretty good judge of character, and I definitely think she's telling the truth about things."

The chief was silent for a long moment. "Fair enough. I had a chat with Lynn upon arrival, and my gut tells me that you're right." He shot her a small smile. "I was just curious as to your assessment of the situation."

"I think there's definitely something odd going on." She considered leaving it at that but decided to put all her cards on the table. "Lori filled me in on what's been going on behind the scenes of the hunt. I know someone was up to no good. But I don't think Lynn had anything to do with it." She smiled. Maybe she could win some brownie points with the chief. "You know, I'm the one who encouraged Lori to contact you in the first place. I felt like you'd want to know what was going on in Sugarcreek."

He raised his eyebrows. "Good to know. Hopefully this time you'll leave things to the professionals. You are strictly here in a 'Lynn's friend' capacity, right?" he asked, making air quotes with his fingers.

"Of course."

"That's what I was hopin' to hear. She'll be glad to see you." He motioned toward the hotel room door. "She's inside. Go on in. We're pretty much done with the crime scene anyway."

Cheryl nodded and hurried off in the direction of the room.

# CHAPTER TWENTY-TWO

Knock, knock," Cheryl said as she pushed the ajar door open. "Anyone here?"

Lynn looked up from where she sat at the table, her face streaked with tears. She looked ten years older than she had earlier. "Thanks for coming."

Cheryl looked around the room. The tidy area she'd seen earlier that day had been replaced by chaos. Pillows and cushions were strewn all over the floor. The contents of the dresser had been removed. There were papers and books tossed about, almost like a tornado had ripped through the room. "Yikes."

"I know. Isn't it terrible?" Lynn asked. "Have a seat if you can find a surface that's intact."

Cheryl picked up a cushion from the floor, put it on the loveseat where it belonged, and sat down. "Do you want to tell me what happened?"

Lynn sighed. "I thought if I could just retrace his steps, I'd find some answers. Instead, no one I spoke to had seen hide nor hair of him. It's like he walked out of this room and just disappeared."

"And you said he left because he had a phone call?" Cheryl asked. She felt a tiny bit guilty at her questioning. Chief Twitchell might accuse her of playing detective if he heard her, but she was genuinely curious and only wanted to help Lynn. Okay, and maybe a small part of her wanted to get to the bottom of everything.

"I didn't actually hear it ring though." Lynn rubbed her temples. "But yes, he said he had to take a call. I guess that could mean he was doing the calling. I don't know that it matters though."

"Well, if we knew who he was talking to or what they were talking about, it might help to know what happened next." Cheryl stood up and paced the now cluttered space. "And do you have any idea what whoever did this may have been looking for?"

Lynn frowned. "Not really. They left my jewelry alone in the bathroom, and there really wasn't anything else of value here. Maybe they were after cash, but I had my purse with me and Gary had his wallet with him. At least I think he did. I didn't see it after he left this morning, so I figure he put it in his pocket like he normally does before he leaves our house in the mornings when he goes to work." The realization that she wasn't totally sure her husband had left with his wallet made her seem even more forlorn than she'd already been.

"Did anyone at the hotel mention if this kind of thing had happened before? Could it possibly have been a coincidence?"

"The manager got here at the same time as the police. She was almost as distraught as me, and she said in all her years of working here, nothing like this had ever happened. So my only guess is that it's somehow connected to Gary. I just can't figure out why." Lynn put her head in her hands again. "I just wish he'd call."

"I'm so sorry." Cheryl knew they must be missing something, but she wasn't sure what. There had to have been something in that room that was worth breaking in to get. Unless it was staged to *look* that way.

"The police have gone through everything here. Now that they're gone, I know I need to force myself to get up and start putting the place back together, but what I really want is just to get out of here."

"I can totally make that happen." Cheryl motioned toward the door. "How about we go grab a cup of coffee? I know just the place."

It took no convincing to get Lynn to leave, although she insisted on leaving a note behind for Gary just in case he returned. "Maybe there's a logical explanation. Do you know that I have actually started to wonder if maybe he told me he was going somewhere and it just didn't register? This whole day is making me crazy."

"I can't even imagine." Cheryl led the way through the hotel lobby and out the front door. A policeman was standing a discreet distance from the front of the hotel, no doubt put there by Chief Twitchell. "Looks like someone is stationed here to watch over things."

"That makes me feel somewhat better. Now if I could just get my Gary back, everything would be okay."

"Have you had the chance to visit the Honey Bee Café yet?" Cheryl asked. "That's where I thought we'd go."

Lynn shook her head. "Not yet, but it was on my list of places I hoped to visit while we were here." Her eyes filled with fresh tears. "I chose it because it sounded like the kind of place Gary would enjoy. He loves finding local places to grab a cup of coffee and a pastry rather than going to a chain."

It seemed at this point, and rightly so, anything Cheryl said might lead back to Lynn thinking about Gary. What were safe topics with a woman whose husband had gone missing? Clearly there are some things that you just couldn't prepare for. "The weather is nice this afternoon, don't you think? It's hard to believe that soon it will look like a fall postcard."

Lynn gave her a tiny smile. "You don't have to try to fill the silence. I'm holding up as well as I can."

"It's that obvious, huh?" Cheryl asked. "Sorry. I just wish I could help you somehow, but I have no idea what to do."

"This is perfect. A little exercise and getting out of the room for a bit. I know Gary wouldn't want me to just sit there and stare at the walls. I have my phone with me so if he calls—or if anyone calls—they can get ahold of me."

They passed the Swiss Miss on the way to the café. "You'll have to stop by tomorrow," Cheryl said. "We have lots of souvenirs and local goods."

"That sounds nice. It looks like such a cute place. This whole town is just so charming. That's one of the reasons I didn't insist on doing our usual Caribbean cruise this year. I thought Sugarcreek and touring Amish country seemed like it would be such a romantic getaway. A place for us to reconnect and just spend time exploring the area together. We've cruised those islands so much that we're pretty much stuck in a rut. Most of the week we're both reading or at one of the trivia events. We kind of do our own thing on those trips. But this. This I thought would be perfect."

"You seem disappointed."

"Aside from the fact that my husband went missing today, he's been acting oddly ever since we got here. Maybe going back to explore roots isn't always what it's cracked up to be."

Cheryl opened the door to the Honey Bee Café and held it while Lynn walked inside. It smelled like freshly baked bread and coffee.

Lynn took a deep breath. "I think I love this place already."

They each ordered coffee—a caramel mocha for Cheryl and a honeycomb latte for Lynn. "I've never had coffee sweetened with honey," said Lynn. "But it sounds pretty yummy to me."

"How about that table by the window?" asked Cheryl, motioning toward an empty table for two.

"Perfect." Lynn led the way to the table and sat down, looking like the weight of the world was on her shoulders. "I feel guilty sitting here drinking a cup of coffee. Maybe I should be out looking for Gary. Maybe I should've stayed at the hotel in case he gets back. What if he's hurt?"

Cheryl couldn't begin to imagine the way she must feel. "We won't stay gone long. You looked as if you might fall apart earlier if you stayed there any longer. Maybe some fresh air will do you some good." She took a sip of her mocha. "I'm sure the police have already asked you several questions, but can you think of anyone who'd want to hurt Gary? Maybe a former student? Or someone he used to know when he visited his family here?"

Lynn shrugged. "I've tried to think of someone who'd want to hurt him, but I can't think of anyone. He really got along with everyone."

Cheryl had her doubts. Gary had been nice enough, but she'd detected a prickly personality. He seemed like the kind of guy who probably rubbed some people the wrong way. But would one of them have been upset enough to follow him to Sugarcreek? Or could it be that he'd met someone in town who'd had an issue with him? "How about you?" Cheryl asked. "Have you given thought to what you'll do now?"

A tear trickled down Lynn's face. "Stay here and wait, I guess. Wait for news from the police. I guess they'll either find him..." Her voice broke. "Or find his body."

Cheryl patted her arm. "I'm sure it won't come to that. I'm praying for the best outcome possible. My friend Naomi is praying too."

"Thank you."

"In the meantime, is there anyone we can call? A family member who can come and stay with you? I hate for you to be alone."

Lynn shook her head. "Our parents are dead. Gary was an only child. My sister is in poor health and lives in Florida. There's no way she could travel here."

"How about extended family?" Cheryl asked. "Cousins? Even a close friend who might come stay with you?" She may not have the largest family in the world, but if there were a crisis, Cheryl knew her parents and her brother would get to her as fast as they could.

"Gary has one cousin, Jimmy, but they haven't spoken in nearly twenty years. Their fathers didn't get along either."

Cheryl frowned. "But what if he knew his cousin was in trouble? Surely he'd care."

"I kind of doubt it. In fact, he might be happy about it." Lynn took a sip of coffee. "Earlier when you asked if Gary got along with everyone? I was serious when I said he did, at least people who are in his life now. But there's only one person in the world I've ever seen Gary fight with." Lynn shook her head. "And I mean it nearly came to blows. I've never seen anything so out of character."

"Why do they dislike each other so much? Just because their dads didn't?" She'd heard stories of family feuds that had begun generations ago and even though later generations didn't even know what the feud was about, they still held the grudge.

Lynn gave her a tiny smile, looked around, and leaned forward. "Gary and Jimmy are locked in a feud over the myth of a buried treasure," she whispered. "Hidden over a hundred years ago."

"What kind of buried treasure?" Cheryl asked, her interest piqued.

"Gold. Lots of gold."

# CHAPTER TWENTY-THREE

G old?" Cheryl hadn't been expecting that.
"That's the legend." Lynn nodded. "Do you want to hear the whole story?"

"Of course." Not only was Cheryl extremely curious, it seemed to be taking Lynn's mind off of her husband. The worried lines had disappeared between her eyes, and she no longer looked like she may burst into sobs at any time.

Lynn shifted in her seat as she prepared to tell the story. "Do you know much about the gold rush in the 1800s?"

Cheryl shrugged. "Only what I learned in a long-ago history class. Gold was discovered at a mill or something and that set off a gold-mining frenzy."

"Basically, yes. At the time, it was the mid-1840s. Gary's great-grandfather, William, and his brother, Horace, set out for the Western frontier. Their parents had died, and they decided to take the trail out West. Horace met a woman along the way and decided to settle down and marry her instead of completing the journey. William left him in Ohio, joined a wagon train, and headed for California."

"Wow. They were really pioneers," Cheryl said, riveted.

"They sure were. Anyway, to hear the family legend, it was definitely the Wild West. William was an entrepreneur even though he was very young. I guess he had a real mind for business. The whole thing happened because of what he considered bad luck at the time though. His wagon broke down, and he was stranded. As it turned out, he was in the right place at the right time. He settled near a little place called Sutter's Mill and opened up a little store. He was just getting his business going when the first gold was found. As people poured into the area to mine for gold, he started selling mining supplies."

"I'll bet that was a lucrative business," Cheryl commented.

Lynn nodded. "Very. If you read up on the history of the gold rush, you'll learn that although the miners made a profit, the business owners in the area made a much larger one. And a lot of the miners paid in gold nuggets."

"That's cool."

"Gary's great-grandpa lived frugally. He stashed the gold and only spent what he had to. He believed it would be the means to living out his dreams. Eventually, as the gold rush began to wind down, he sold his business, packed up his gold, and started the treacherous trek east. He and Horace had written letters to one another over the years, and William's dream was to move to where his brother's family lived."

"Travel was so hard back then. It's a wonder he made it." Cheryl had a sudden flashback to playing an Oregon Trail computer game in elementary school and dying of dysentery or measles or something else horrible.

Lynn took a sip of coffee. "He almost didn't. He got very sick on the way and ran into some weather that I can't imagine being exposed to. There weren't Holiday Inns and Walgreens on every corner along the route, you know? It really was a different time." She smiled. "But his illness also brought him the woman who would become his wife. He was taken in by a group who took pity on him, and one of the men had a daughter who had a knack for medicine. She had lots of natural home remedies for things that her grandmother had taught her. She nursed him back to health. Her name was Lola, and by the time they reached Ohio, she was William's wife."

"That's sweet."

"The sad part of the story, though, is that by the time they arrived in Ohio, Horace and his wife were both dead. There was a flu epidemic that winter, and the whole family perished."

Cheryl slumped in her seat. "After William and Lola got married, I was expecting a happy reunion with the rest of the family." What a sad story it had turned out to be.

"Sadly, that's not the case. William was heartbroken, but Lola did what she could to cheer him up. They built a home just outside of Sugarcreek—called Shanesville at that time—and had two sons. One of their sons, Walt, would turn out to be Gary's grandpa. The other son, Simon, would be Jimmy's."

"And are they the ones the feud began with?" Cheryl asked.

Lynn nodded. "Yes. It all started with the two of them. They were close together in age and when they were young, they were best friends. There was a girl named Victoria who lived at the nearest farm to theirs, and the three of them were inseparable."

Cheryl could see where this may be going. "Why do I get the feeling this is going to be a sad story?"

"You'd be feeling right." Lynn sighed. "As you may have guessed, both Walt and Simon fell in love with Victoria. The boys competed for her affections when they were in their teens, but she would never declare her love for either of them—not even when they both left home to fight in the Civil War."

"It's like a tragic love story."

"When they left, the boys were embroiled in their own war. They'd fought over Victoria so much, they couldn't get back to being friends and behaving as brothers should. They joined different regiments and left home hating each other." Lynn shook her head. "It was an awful time for their parents anyway, made worse by the fact that their beloved sons were so nasty to one another. Midway through the war, both boys came home on furlough at the same time because by then William and Lola were old and in poor health."

"What about Victoria? Did she see them again?"

Lynn smiled. "The heart of a teenage girl was fickle even then. Victoria married while they were away. She treasured the friendship they'd shared throughout their childhood, and I don't think she would've ever chosen one brother over the other. She and their parents thought her marriage would be the end of the boys' feud."

"But they were wrong."

"Sadly, yes. Somehow her marriage only made them resent each other more. I guess maybe each thought if it hadn't been for the other one, she would've waited. Based on a letter I've read that Lola wrote back then, the boys were horrible to one another during that furlough and it just about broke their parents' hearts. When they left to return to the battlefield, Lola wrote to a friend and said she and William feared they wouldn't live to see their sons again...and she was right. William and Lola passed away within a week of each other the week before the war ended."

Cheryl frowned and shook her head. "That's so sad. Those poor parents."

Lynn nodded. "Yes. But William and Lola devised a plan before they died. They'd always planned to leave the gold to Walt and Simon. William had been frugal, and Lola was a thrifty housewife. They hardly used any of William's stash of gold, wanting instead to leave it as an inheritance for their sons."

"So what happened?"

"Before they died, William and Lola hid the gold. They made a map, and on the map, they wrote a riddle. Then they tore it in half." Lynn smiled. "I always liked that. So clever of them. It would've been easy to just divvy up the gold and let their sons go their separate ways. But William had known the love of a brother. He never got over his brother, Horace, dying before they could be reunited. His great pleasure was seeing how close his own sons were. So when the rift occurred and kept getting worse, he knew he needed to do something drastic."

"That makes sense."

"When Walt and Simon returned home from the war and found their parents had died, they expected a great inheritance. Instead, each of them received half a map and an identical letter. The letter was from William and Lola, pleading with them to mend their relationship and live in harmony. The only way to find the hidden gold would be to work together—to put their map halves together so they could see the whole map and read the whole riddle."

"But they wouldn't do it? Not even for gold?"

"Can you say stubborn?" Lynn grinned. "I can't tell you how many times I've reminded Gary that he was just like the rest of the men in his family—stubborn as a mule."

"What happened next?"

"They never reconciled. They sold the home place and split the profits—although I think even doing that caused them to argue. They each moved away, married, and each had a son very late in life. Walt's son, Jack, was Gary's father. Simon's son, Luke, was Jimmy's father."

"So what's the year at this point?" Cheryl was trying to place the family saga against a historical backdrop.

"Early 1900s. Jack and Luke were cousins, although they only met once or twice. Their fathers had poisoned them against each other, so they never really had a chance to be friends. Their mothers, however, tried to reunite the family. Apparently it was disastrous, and they never tried again."

Cheryl shook her head. "So many people have no family and would jump at the chance to have one. But they chose to stay estranged even though the feud had nothing to do with them."

"I can't tell you how many times I've said that very thing." Lynn took the last sip of her coffee. "Just as their fathers had, Jack and Luke refused to work together to find the gold. Walt and

Simon had each passed their half of the map to their own son." She shook her head. "But it didn't matter. Gary and Jimmy were both born in the 1940s just after World War II ended. In most families, they would've come together and celebrated these two new baby boys who should've grown up together and been close friends."

"And that didn't happen."

Lynn shook her head. "No it did not. What started as a feud between Walt and Simon over a girl who'd gone on to marry someone else continued with Jack and Luke. They could never see eye to eye on anything—including whether to work together to find the family fortune."

"And then Gary and Jimmy grew up disliking each other as well."

"It was not for my lack of trying. I encouraged them to get together and reconcile this silly feud. Twenty years ago, we met Jimmy for dinner. The two of them were so much alike it was comical. Or it would've been if they'd gotten along." She shook her head. "Gary's mom's family is close, thank goodness. He's had a normal familial relationship with them—he and a cousin are even colleagues at the university. But Jimmy... Jimmy and Gary are still at odds."

"And they're the last of the line?" Cheryl was pretty sure Lynn had mentioned that they didn't have children.

"I have always felt like their family's legacy of discord is the reason neither of them desired children of their own. Jimmy was married a long time ago, but his wife passed away and they never had children. I knew when I met Gary that he didn't want to have children, and I was okay with that. We've had a full life together with friends and family, and that has been enough for us."

"So they are the last ones then? The map halves, the family gold…It all just…" Cheryl had been about to say "dies with them," but she realized how upsetting that might be to a woman whose husband was missing. "It just ends?"

"Yes. Gary and I have never really discussed it. There'd be no point in leaving his half to someone else. Without Jimmy's half, it wouldn't make any sense."

"So you haven't seen or heard from Jimmy in twenty years?"

Lynn shook her head. "No. I'm not sure I'd even recognize him now." She gave a small smile. "Actually I might. He carries a very ornate pocket watch that belonged to William. He's kept it in pristine condition all these years. I think he had it restored. It worked and everything. Last time we saw him, he made a point to pull it out several times just to rub it in Gary's face." She grinned. "What he doesn't know is that Gary got William's pistol and that means as much to him as the watch would've."

"Such a shame for two men who obviously care a great deal about their family history to be so estranged."

"I know. I've prayed for years that the two of them would reconcile and finally end this family feud while they're still in good enough health to enjoy one another's company. I suspect they have a lot in common and could be great friends if they'd allow themselves to be."

Cheryl nodded. "I'll pray for the same outcome. And for Gary to return to you safe and sound—and soon."

# CHAPTER TWENTY-FOUR

Cheryl's mind was still reeling later that night when she arrived to the scavenger hunt meeting. She waved Levi over as soon as she spotted him.

"Tough day?" he asked softly.

"I guess Naomi told you what happened?"

He nodded, his blue eyes serious. "Ja. If you can think of any way for me and my family to help, let us know."

"I'll pass that along to Lynn. I think she wants to organize a search party tomorrow if he hasn't been found or tried to contact her."

"Are there any leads?" he asked.

Cheryl shook her head. "Honestly, I don't know. I saw Chief Twitchell earlier, but he didn't say anything other than ask me if I thought Lynn could somehow be involved."

He raised his eyebrows. "And do you?"

She was quiet for a moment. "At first I considered it. I mean, two people from out of town who don't know anyone here and then one goes missing. I think any detective worth their weight would have to at least consider the remaining person as a suspect. But I spent time with her right after his disappearance and again after the hotel room was ransacked. She's terrified of living without him. They've clung to each other through the years—over friends and over family. From her story, they are each other's worlds. I think she's genuinely concerned for his safety and not even letting herself imagine an outcome where they don't leave Sugarcreek together and go back home. So I don't think she was involved."

"I pray he comes back to her safe and sound." He leveled his eyes on her. "And that you do not get involved. The police are capable of locating him and determining what happened."

Cheryl nodded. "Of course." She fully intended to let Chief Twitchell handle the situation. That wasn't to say that she hadn't been going over the facts though. She couldn't help but wonder if the strange happenings with the flyers and the clue cards might somehow be related to Gary's disappearance.

"Thanks for coming, everyone," Lori said from her spot at the front of the crowd. "Can you believe it's time for the final clue?"

The crowd clapped.

"Tonight's meeting will be brief," she said. "But important." She grinned. "First I want to congratulate our final five teams for making it this far. From the feedback you all have given me, I think you've all had a lot of fun and I'm so glad." She grew serious. "However, due to an emergency, one of our teams has had to drop out of the hunt. Please keep the Calloways in your thoughts and prayers, as Gary left his hotel this morning and hasn't been seen or heard from since."

Murmurs rippled through the crowd. Gary's disappearance hadn't been common knowledge, so many of the townspeople were just hearing about it.

"Are we in danger?" one woman asked. "Is there something sinister happening?"

Lori shook her head. "I don't think you have anything to worry about. Chief Twitchell from the Sugarcreek Police Department is here to say a few words."

The chief made his way to the front of the crowd and stood next to Lori. "First of all, I want to assure each of you that there is no need to fear for your safety. What happened this mornin' appears to have been an isolated incident, and we are lookin' into Mr. Calloway's background for answers. The citizens of Sugarcreek can help us though. If any of you have any information about Mr. Calloway or his disappearance, I ask that you come see me after the meeting or come to the station and give a statement. I am confident that we will get Mr. Calloway back safe and unharmed." He paused as the crowd applauded. "I ask that everyone continue to keep an eye out, and if you see anything suspicious, let me know. Your Sugarcreek Police Department is always here to help." With a nod of his head, he stepped away from the podium and made his way to a spot toward the back of the bleachers.

The crowd chattered as Lori tried to regain control. "Thanks for your cooperation with Chief Twitchell. He'll be around for a while, so if anyone has anything to discuss with him, please do so." She turned her attention to a sheet of paper on the podium. "Without further ado, here's your final clue:

"You've all searched low.
You've all searched high.

And now it's time
to say good-bye.
At the final stop
there are no dragons.
It's where you go
to ride a wagon."

Several members of the crowd whispered to their neighbors.

Cheryl and Levi looked at one another and shrugged. "You can ride a wagon pretty much anywhere," whispered Levi.

"And I don't think there are any dragons around." It was a pretty vague clue. But it was clear they were trying to make the final hunt a little tougher than the last.

"Ladies and gentleman, the clue will be open for hunting on Wednesday at 5:00 p.m., which gives you tomorrow to plan your attack." She grinned. "That's all for tonight. Help yourself to some refreshments, and please join us on Thursday evening at six o'clock for the wrap-up party. We'll be announcing the winner of the one-thousand-dollar grand prize, and Mr. Arnold, the sponsor of the whole event, will be here to present the winners' check and thank everyone for participating." She grinned. "And come hungry. Log Cabin Catering is going to provide us with some yummy food."

Cheryl made a mental note to bring Julia with her on Thursday. Log Cabin Catering had done the food for an event she'd attended a couple of months ago, and it was delicious. The other treasure hunt meetings had offered standard finger foods—chips and dip, sausage balls, and brownies—but if Log Cabin was catering on Thursday, it would be a full meal. She stood and followed the crowd down the bleachers. The line at the refreshment table was already lengthy. She glanced around to see if anyone was talking to the chief, but she didn't see him anywhere. She grabbed a copy of the clue sheet from the podium and handed it to Levi then took one for herself.

"Are you staying to eat?" Levi asked.

She shook her head. "After the crazy day I had, I really just want to get home." Not only did she want to phone Lynn to see how she was holding up, but she also needed to have a serious talk with Julia. "There's been so much going on."

"I understand." Levi was quiet for a moment. "I know things seem dark now, Cheryl. But it is always darkest before the dawn." He smiled. "Daed has said that for as long as I can remember, and in every situation it has turned out to be right."

"He's a wise man."

"I have some Bible covers done for the shop. I meant to bring them by today, but things were busy at the farm. I will bring them tomorrow afternoon, and we can discuss the final clue." He smiled and held up the sheet with the clue written on it. "I promised Maam I would bring this home. She may come with us to hunt, especially if she has an idea as to where it is."

"Sounds wonderful." Cheryl told him good-bye and turned to go.

"Cheryl!" someone called.

She turned to see Grace rushing toward her.

"Isn't it just awful about Mr. Calloway?" Grace asked. "I heard about it just before we left for the meeting. I ran by the grocery store, and there was a lady in there talking about it. I guess she works at the hotel where he was staying. She said he just disappeared into thin air." She furrowed her brow. "But there must be more to it than that."

"It is truly awful. His wife, Lynn, is very distraught."

"I can't imagine. If something happened to James, I think I would fall apart."

Cheryl nodded. "I know. I hope that tomorrow brings answers."

"Are you leaving now?" Grace asked. "You aren't staying for refreshments?"

Cheryl shook her head. "I have some things to do at home." She grinned. "But I'll stay on Thursday night. It sounds like we're in for a real treat from Log Cabin."

"Definitely. See you then! And good luck with the final clue." Grace went back to where James stood talking to Levi.

Cheryl walked to her car, lost in thought. The clue didn't make sense to her so far, but maybe it would come together. She turned her mind to Julia and how to handle the situation. If she outright asked about the passport application, Julia may think she'd been snooping through her stuff. But she needed to bring it up.

She was still considering it when she pulled into the driveway at home.

The house was dark.

Unless Julia had gone out with someone—her car was in the driveway—it looked like their conversation would have to wait. The whole time Julia had been there, she hadn't turned in this early. It was just Cheryl's luck that when she'd finally decided to confront her, she'd be in bed.

She walked inside, and Beau met her at the door. He tried unsuccessfully to trip her twice before she could get to his food bowl in the kitchen. "Silly boy. If you break my leg, who will take care of you while I recover?"

He ignored her and turned his attention to the food she'd put in his bowl.

She noticed a note on the kitchen table.

*Leftovers in the fridge. Chicken potpie. It's not my best, but I thought you might be hungry. See you in the morning. Julia.*

Julia's time in Sugarcreek was winding down. In less than a week, she'd be leaving for Ohio State. Not only would Cheryl miss having someone to come home to, she'd also miss having someone cook for her. They'd barely eaten out for dinner, what with Julia's love of cooking. And there'd been desserts aplenty too. It had been like living with Betty Crocker as a houseguest. Cheryl patted her midsection. She had the extra pounds to prove it too.

She put a slice of potpie on a plate and stuck it in the microwave. It looked delicious.

She grabbed her bag and fished around for the clue sheet. The book she'd taken from the Calloways' hotel room was still in there. She'd been so busy, she'd forgotten to go by the library. That could go on her to-do list for tomorrow.

The microwave dinged, and Cheryl took her plate and the book to the kitchen table. She flipped through the book. As old books do, it had a musty smell and yellowing pages. She read a chapter on the settling of Sugarcreek—it was first called Shanesville—and tried to imagine being the first people to inhabit an area. How different the landscape must have been then.

An old parchment fell out of the middle of the book, and she unfolded it.

Her heart pounded.

She was holding what must be Gary's copy of the old family map.

It had been ripped in two and was faded with age, but she could still see Walt Calloway's name written on the top.

The left half of the map showed a boundary that she guessed was Sugarcreek. It seemed familiar to her, although she couldn't figure out why.

There were words scrawled in old-fashioned handwriting below the map. It was some kind of riddle, undoubtedly giving a clue as to where the gold was hidden:

A place

A place

Some goods

Some goods

It's always

And cool

To find

Search

She could see how William and Lola had ensured their sons would have to work together to solve the puzzle. Half of the clue was meaningless without the other half. How disappointed would they be to know that three generations had passed and the reconciliation hadn't happened? She suspected they'd be devastated to see how their family remained divided.

She needed to give this map back to Lynn. She must've had no idea it had been stashed in the book.

But first she needed to make a copy of it. She grabbed her phone and took a photo of the paper and took another that zoomed in on the words. Not that she thought she'd ever search for the gold herself, but she wouldn't mind trying to figure out the puzzle.

The ring of the home phone cut through the silent house like a siren.

Cheryl raced to the receiver before it woke Julia.

And prayed it wasn't bad news.

# CHAPTER TWENTY-FIVE

Ello?" a heavily accented male voice said. "Could I speak to Julia?"

Cheryl paused. "She can't come to the phone right now. Can I take a message?"

"No zank you. I vill call for her again later." The phone clicked off.

Cheryl stared at the receiver. She was beginning to realize that Julia was full of secrets.

And although she intended to get to the bottom of them, she'd have to wait another day. She had other things to tend to now.

She dialed Lynn's cell number.

Lynn picked up on the first ring. "Hello."

"It's Cheryl."

"Oh." The disappointment in her voice was evident. "Thanks for calling. Still no news."

"I just wanted to make sure you're okay. Let me know if there's anything I can do."

There was a long pause on the other end. "I want to search for Gary tomorrow afternoon. The police say they are on top of things, but I'd feel better if I knew I'd done all I could do. Can you help me get some volunteers together to look around the immediate area?" Her voice broke. "I keep imagining him out there somewhere hurt and stranded."

"Of course. I'll get people together tomorrow afternoon, and we'll help you search. I'll call you when I have some volunteers."

"Thanks, Cheryl. It will help me rest easier knowing we can look for ourselves tomorrow."

"Call me if there's anything new or if you need anything," Cheryl said.

She hung up the phone and sat down in the recliner. Where could Gary be? She flipped through her phone until she got to the photo of his map. She'd forgotten to tell Lynn she had it. Oh well, she'd tell her tomorrow. It might only upset her at this point.

She peered closely at the side of the map boundary. It wasn't Sugarcreek, but it looked so familiar. Where had she seen it before?

Suddenly she jumped up and ran to the kitchen. She riffled through the papers she'd stacked there last week until she found the papers from the very first treasure hunt meeting. She flipped through until she found the boundary map Lori had given them that showed where the clues could be hidden. The left boundary exactly matched Gary's map. Lori had said the map she gave them contained a certain radius around Sugarcreek.

And that radius appeared to perfectly match the map William Caldwell had drawn over one hundred years ago.

Cheryl's mind raced as she considered what that might mean. She returned to the living room and settled in, leaning her head against the recliner to think. Was it possible that Gary's family gold and the treasure hunt were connected somehow? Before she could follow that train of thought any further, Julia walked into the room.

"I woke up and heard you in the kitchen," she said. "So I thought I'd come make sure you found the apple dumplings I made earlier." She grinned. "Plus I was kind of hungry for one too."

"I didn't have one yet," Cheryl said as she stood up. "But that sounds delicious." She followed Julia into the kitchen, wishing she'd taken more time rehearsing what she wanted to say to the girl. "The potpie was very good too. Thanks for doing that."

Julia looked pleased. "You're welcome. It's the least I can do for you to let me stay here." She pulled a container out of the refrigerator. "You can eat them cold, but they'll be better heated. There's some caramel sauce to drizzle on top, and I got some vanilla ice cream to go with it."

Now certainly wasn't the time to start counting calories, but as soon as Julia left for school, Cheryl was going to have to get back on track. "Sounds great." She pulled two bowls out of the cabinet and set them next to the container.

Julia scooped an apple dumpling into each bowl and placed them in the microwave. "They're very easy to make. And that little produce stand—Sweetwater Farms—had the tastiest apples." She took the bowls out of the microwave and drizzled caramel sauce on top of each dumpling.

"No ice cream for me," Cheryl said. "I have to cut corners somewhere."

Julia giggled. "I know, right?"

They took their bowls and sat down at the table.

Cheryl took a bite. "This is amazing. The pastry is flaky and perfect."

"Thanks. These are one of my favorite things to make. I love the blend of caramel and apple and cinnamon. This is like the epitome of comfort food for me."

They ate in silence for a few minutes. Finally, Cheryl couldn't wait any longer.

"I think we need to talk."

Julia put her spoon down and looked up, a surprised expression on her face. "What about?"

"I hope you won't think I'm overstepping here, but there are some things I'm concerned about." Cheryl's heart beat faster. She hated confrontation, especially when she wasn't sure her input would be welcome.

"Okay. Like what?" Julia twirled a strand of hair that had come loose from her messy bun.

"Last week there was a letter from Ohio State in the hallway. I picked it up thinking it was trash. When I looked at it, I saw that it was your scholarship letter. You'd checked the box to decline your scholarship." She leveled her gaze on Julia. "What's that about? I thought you and your mom both told me what a great scholarship package you'd received and how happy you both were to get it."

Julia shifted in her seat, an uncomfortable look on her face. "If it makes you feel any better, I haven't mailed it in yet. It's sitting in my room in the envelope."

"I don't know that it makes me feel better, but at least I don't feel like you came to my house and declined your scholarship without your parents knowing about it."

"For all I know, Mom has already gone online and accepted it for me. I wouldn't put it past her. She even filled out my application for housing, including all my likes and dislikes that they use to match up roommates."

Cheryl was horrified but tried not to let on. Michelle had come across as overbearing when they spoke, but this seemed more than a little overboard. "I went in your room to get your dirty towels to throw in the wash. I didn't go through your stuff, so please don't think that. But I saw a US passport application on the desk."

Julia sat stone-faced, but didn't say anything.

"And then earlier tonight a man called here asking for you. He had a heavy accent."

At that, Julia sat up straighter. "Really? Did he leave a message?"

"He'll call back." Cheryl sighed. "But can you please tell me what's going on?"

Julia put her head in her hands. "I don't even know where to start." She looked up with tears in her eyes. "My mom and dad have had my life planned out for me for as long as I can remember. I mentioned last year that I'd like to visit some schools to know what my options were. You'd have thought I said I was going to shave my head and get tattoos all over my body. My mom went a little nuts. She said there was no need to look anywhere else and that I would love it at OSU. I tried to convince myself that she was right, but I don't think she is."

"So you don't want to go there?"

Julia shook her head. "Not even a little bit. Trevor and I have been fighting about it all summer. He knows how I feel, and he thinks I'm crazy. I got a good scholarship, and he says this will be the adventure of a lifetime."

"But you don't think so. Is there a different school you want to go to?"

"Kind of." Julia sighed. "It's complicated."

Dealing with teenagers may not be her strength. Cheryl patted Julia's hand. "Try me."

"I just don't see the point in spending the time and money going to school when I already know what I want to do with my life." She smiled. A tiny smile but a smile nevertheless. "You know how I love to cook?"

"Yeah," Cheryl said.

"That's what I want to do. I've tried to tell my parents for two years now, but they won't listen. I love cooking for people. And I think I'm good at it. I create new recipes, and I improve on old ones. This is what I'm meant to do," she said as she held up her empty apple dumpling bowl.

"Have you talked seriously to your parents about your future? Maybe they don't know you want to pursue a career in culinary arts—maybe they think it's just a hobby." Cheryl hated the thought of Julia's parents not supporting her dreams.

"They won't listen. Mom's heart is set on me following her footsteps and having a career in marketing and public relations. But we are so different. I'm terrible at the stuff she's good at. She forced me to go out for cheerleading in junior high, and it was a total disaster. I felt like such a disappointment to her."

"I can promise you that your mom is in no way disappointed in you. The few times I've spoken to her, she has been so proud to tell me about your accomplishments and her hopes for your future. She may be a little more involved than you'd like, but she is definitely not disappointed."

Julia let out a huge sigh. "I don't know what to do. I'm all set to decline my scholarship and go to culinary school. I can take out a student loan to cover the cost. But I'm terrified to stand up to my parents. That man who called tonight was probably from the culinary school in France that I've been in contact with. They've trained some top pastry chefs, and I think I'd love it."

"So that's what the passport application is for? Because you want to ditch Ohio State and head to culinary school?" Cheryl had to admit, the girl was ambitious. Most eighteen-year-olds were scared to head to college, much less travel out of the country and attend school.

"Yeah. I just can't quite pull the trigger on my plan without my parents giving me their blessing. I wish I was one of those kids who could, but I'd feel so guilty I'd never even be able to enjoy it." She frowned. "I'd hoped staying here for a couple of weeks would give me the answer."

"So that's why you're here. I kind of wondered what you were really doing in Amish country at my house for the two weeks leading up to college." Chery grinned. "I mean, I'm glad to have you, but I was surprised."

Julia shrugged. "That isn't the whole reason I'm here. I mean, you're kind of my hero."

Cheryl widened her eyes. "I'm your hero? How so?" She was completely flattered, but seeing as how she'd only just met Julia two weeks ago, she couldn't imagine how she could be considered a hero.

"You took control of your life. You left your safe banking job and followed your heart. Some of the family thought you were nuts, you know. Moving to some small town and taking over a gift shop when you had no background in running a business? That seemed crazy to a lot of them. And leaving a steady income for the unknown was a pretty big leap of faith." She smiled. "I always think of you when I consider my own future. For me, going into marketing and public relations would be like you staying in banking. Maybe safe, but not where my heart is. And I think when you get to a certain point in life, you need to follow your own heart and your own dreams." She shrugged. "I want to do that just like you did."

Although Cheryl wanted to ask which family members had thought her to be nuts, now wasn't the time. "Well, I'm very flattered you feel that way, but remember that I was much older than you. I had some money saved up and had just gotten out of a relationship that I thought was going to lead to marriage. So my move to Sugarcreek was definitely a leap of faith, but it was also a different circumstance. I do see what you mean though." She gave her a sideways glance. "How about Trevor? How does he figure in to all of this?"

Julia wrinkled her nose. "He is 100 percent not supportive. I told him it was my dream to first be a chef in a restaurant and eventually open up my own after I have some experience under my belt. He thinks the whole thing is crazy. He doesn't get why I'd go into a field where I'd have to work nights and weekends rather than just a standard eight-to-five kind of thing."

"So he doesn't get that it's your dream." Cheryl could see the hurt on Julia's face when she talked about it. It genuinely hurt Julia that her boyfriend didn't support her dreams and want her to follow them. And frankly Cheryl didn't blame her.

"Not at all. He doesn't get the concept of a career you're passionate about. He's only interested in drawing a salary, and that's about it. He plans to just get a degree in accounting so he can always find a job."

Cheryl pondered her next words for a moment.

She wasn't sure she was the best person to give advice on love and life, but she'd give it her best shot.

# CHAPTER TWENTY-SIX

"Trevor is only eighteen," Cheryl began. "It's entirely possible that he just hasn't found what he's passionate about yet. Most people don't know at eighteen what they want to do with their lives. I certainly didn't. You're lucky that you've discovered such a talent and that it happens to be for something that you love to do. Don't be too hard on him for deciding on a major because someone in his family has that career. He very well may change his mind once he gets to college and starts to figure out who he really is."

"That could happen, I guess," Julia said glumly.

"Or maybe your trouble with Trevor has nothing to do with his lack of ambition or what major he's going to pick. Maybe it's just that he's not the right guy for you. Or maybe he's the right guy, but this is the wrong time."

"But what do I do?"

The worst part about becoming an adult was that you could no longer rely on someone else to make your decisions for you. You had to decide for yourself. "I think this is one of those times when you have to decide what you want. And then you have to go for it."

Julia nodded. "I thought so."

"Sorry things are tough." Cheryl felt nothing but sympathy for Julia. She was caught somewhere between a child and an adult, and she was going to have to face a hard lesson—sometimes going after your dreams and doing what was best for you would end up hurting other people.

"Me too." Julia managed a tiny smile. "But you've been really helpful. I'm sorry I sort of hid out here while I was dealing with all of this. I just knew if I stayed at home, I'd let my mom talk me into going down the path that she's always hoped I'd choose." She shook her head. "But that's not what I want. I think it's time I come clean with my parents and with Trevor. They need to know once and for all how important pursuing my passion is. They may not totally support my decisions, but I hope they will accept them."

"Do you want to call your mom now? You're welcome to invite your parents here if you'd like." Cheryl hoped she wouldn't regret that invitation, but she got the feeling Julia may need someone in her corner.

"Thanks. I'd like that." Julia stood. "I'm going to go call them now and see if they can come a few days early."

"And Trevor?"

Julia sighed. "I think it's time for Trevor and me to part ways. He deserves someone who is 100 percent sure about him, and I'm not that girl." She turned to go.

"Good luck."

Julia turned back around and smiled. "I've been praying about it just like you said. I'd already pretty much reached a decision before talking to you tonight. There's a big feeling of peace when I lean one direction and only turmoil in the other. I believe that's the answer."

Cheryl watched her go and considered all the events of the day. From the first phone call from Lynn to the ransacked room to the treasure hunt meeting…there had been so many questions but few answers. At least the questions surrounding Julia had been answered.

The next morning, Cheryl woke up early. She'd tossed and turned all night, never quite finding herself able to completely rest.

She got ready for work quickly and left a note for Julia on the table. *Come to the shop this afternoon if you can. We're going to be searching for Mr. Calloway and can use all the help we can get.*

She grabbed the library book from Gary and Lynn's room and put it in her bag. Something was nagging at her, but she couldn't figure out what. She poured Beau a scoop of food. "How about you stay here today, okay, buddy? There's way too much going on for you to be at the shop." She knew she may be in and out and would hate to have a repeat of yesterday and have to go back to the shop to get Beau. He hated staying there alone, and at least here he could just go curl up in bed. She scratched him behind the ears then headed out the door.

Once she opened the store, she poured herself a cup of coffee and sat down at the counter with the library book. She flipped through it, looking for any reference to buried gold, but found none.

Maybe it was time to make a list of everything she knew. She pulled out a pencil and a notepad and wrote:

1. Fake flyers
2. Library clue mix-up
3. Gary: phone calls, stress
4. Map
5. Disappearance

She picked up her phone and called Lori. Hopefully the girl wouldn't still be sleeping.

Lori answered on the third ring. "Hello?"

"Lori? It's Cheryl Cooper. Sorry to bother you, but something you told me last week has me curious."

"What's that?" Lori asked.

"You told me that whoever put out those fake flyers only put them in one location. Where was it? Where did you see the flyers?"

Lori was quiet for a moment. "They were near that little antique shop that has a toy train in the window."

"The antique shop that's next door to the hotel?"

"Yeah. There were some flyers there too. In fact, I went inside, and there was even one posted at the front desk of the hotel."

So the fake flyers had only been put up in the area where Gary and Lynn were staying. That couldn't be a coincidence. "Thanks so much, Lori."

They said good-bye and hung up.

Cheryl wrote Gary's name next to *fake flyers* on her list. So it was entirely possible that the flyers had been put out to throw Gary and Lynn off...or to get them to visit a different location than the one they were supposed to go to. On a hunch, she called Lynn. She didn't want to alarm her though, so she tried to keep her voice steady.

Lynn answered immediately. "Have you heard anything?" she asked frantically.

Cheryl sort of wished she hadn't bothered her, knowing the distress she was in, but it had to be done. "No," she said. "I wanted to touch base about this afternoon. I'm going to get people together, and I thought we'd just meet at the Swiss Miss and then walk to your hotel as a group. Is that okay?"

"Oh. Yes, that's fine."

"Great. And I have one thing to ask you. The other day when you and Gary found the Agatha Christie clue in the library, what did your clue say?"

"I don't have time to worry about the treasure hunt now." Lynn's words were clipped.

"Please don't be upset. I'm trying to help. I don't think any of the groups got the same clue. I just wondered if maybe the clue you and Gary got might be helpful in tracking down whoever was trying to sabotage the hunt."

"Oh." Her voice was more relaxed now. "Well, I can't speak for Gary, but my clue was mostly nonsense."

Cheryl raised an eyebrow. "Hold on. You and Gary had separate clues?"

Lynn sighed. "Yes. Didn't everyone? There was one envelope with our names on it, but that envelope contained two separate envelopes. There were instructions for us not to share clues with each other or we'd be disqualified. It's odd, but we wanted to play the game right."

"Do you know where Gary's clue is?"

"He had it stuck in his pocket yesterday morning when he left the hotel. I told him he was silly because it was a fake clue, but he seemed to think it was something he should hold on to. I have no idea what it said."

"Okay. Well, don't worry about it. I'm sure it was nothing important." Cheryl tried to hide her disappointment. She'd hoped that whatever Gary's clue had said might give her some lead on where he was or who he was with.

"I still have mine though," Lynn said. "I stuck it in my purse or whoever ransacked our room probably would've taken it with all the other papers they took."

Cheryl pressed the phone harder against her ear. "I didn't know they took papers." She was sure Lynn hadn't mentioned that yesterday.

"I only realized it last night when I was cleaning up. The notes and stuff Gary had made when he was digging through that old history book were all gone."

"Oh, I'm glad you mentioned the book!" Cheryl said. "The map. Gary's great-grandpa's map. It was inside the book. I guess he'd stuck it there."

Lynn sniffled. "It is? Well, I'm glad you found it before you returned the book. He'd be so upset if he lost that." She sniffled again. "I'll get it back from you this afternoon."

"Of course." Cheryl had left the copy of the map at her house. It was a valuable document just from a historic standpoint, and she hadn't wanted it to get messed up while it was in her possession. She'd go get it at lunch.

"Hold on, and I'll read you what my clue said. It was just a bunch of gibberish."

Cheryl grinned at her use of the word. It reminded her of something her grandma used to say. "Take your time."

"Okay, here goes. It's really just a bunch of words. It says, 'Time to end this. To store to stow you buy you grow dark year-round this place underground." Lynn took a breath. "See? No sense at all."

Cheryl jotted down the words. "No worries. My clue was blank. So at least yours had some words." She had no idea what Lynn's clue meant. It could be "gibberish" just like she'd said. "Did Gary look at your clue?"

"No. It's like I said. We thought the clues were real and didn't want to break the rules. We were already in bed that night when Lori called us with the real clue. And the next morning early, yesterday, Gary left the room and didn't come back. So we didn't really get the chance to discuss the clues that turned out to be fake."

"Gotcha. Okay. Well, if there are any new developments, give me a call. Otherwise, we'll be there this afternoon."

Lynn thanked her and hung up.

Before Cheryl could focus any more on the mystery at hand, the store got busy. Esther wasn't scheduled to come in until later, so Cheryl had to put all her attention toward her customers.

Finally just before noon, there was a lull.

She normally never closed the store for lunch—she and Esther or one of the other girls would work it out so there was always someone there. But today Cheryl needed some time to think. She turned the sign to the Closed position and went back to her notes.

She pulled out her phone and flipped to the photo of Gary's map. Although she couldn't be sure without looking at the actual map again, it seemed like there may be a spot marked on the map itself. From what she could see, the rest of the marking would lie on the other map half. It was possible that would give the actual location of the gold.

Cheryl read over the words again. Without their counterparts, they were totally meaningless. She stared at them for another minute.

A place

A place

Some goods

Some goods

It's always

And cool

To find

Search

Where could it be referencing? She put her head in her hands and closed her eyes. She was missing something.

The answer hit her like a ton of bricks. She flipped through the papers till she found the random words from Lynn's clue cards.

The riddle was now intact.

And Cheryl knew who had taken Gary.

His cousin Jimmy.

# CHAPTER TWENTY-SEVEN

With trembling fingers, Cheryl wrote out the entire clue then looked at her work.

> A place to store
> A place to stow
> Some goods you buy
> Some goods you grow
> It's always dark
> And cool year-round
> To find this place
> Search underground

This was it! The riddle that had been waiting for more than a century to be solved. Cheryl could barely contain her excitement. Who should she call first? Lynn? Chief Twitchell?

It wasn't lost on her that her first thought was she wished Levi had a cell phone.

A tap on the door brought her back to reality.

Levi.

She couldn't keep the goofy grin off her face as she unlocked the door. "You're not going to believe it!" she exclaimed.

Levi burst out laughing. "You look like the cat who ate the canary. And why is the Swiss Miss closed in the middle of the day?"

"I had some things to tend to." She pulled him down the aisle. "I think I know who has Gary," she said proudly.

Levi widened his eyes. "I am not surprised by that, but why do not you start at the beginning?"

She nodded. "Okay." She explained the whole story to him, from the lost gold to the clues to the map. "Gary's cousin Jimmy is behind it. He has to be. And now *I* have the whole clue too. Read this." She thrust the paper at him that she'd written the riddle on. "What do you think?"

"I am not sure."

She reread the riddle. "It stands to reason that this wouldn't be anything difficult to find. The whole point was for the boys to come together and share the map and find it together. It must be a location on the old Calloway property."

"Where is that?" Levi asked.

She wrinkled her nose. "That's the part I don't know. But off the top of my head, I'd say this is some kind of underground storage area. Remember this was meant to be found back in the 1800s. Gary and Jimmy's great-grandparents didn't expect generations to pass before any of their family came to find their inheritance. Back then an underground storage would've been common."

Levi nodded. "Like a cellar. A root cellar."

"That's it, I'll bet!" Cheryl exclaimed.

"But Jimmy does not have the rest of the clue, right? So he would have no way of knowing the answer to the riddle."

She nodded. "Right. Not unless Gary had it memorized. Because I know Gary didn't have his part of the map and riddle with him—that's at my house."

"So we still do not know where to look for Gary."

Cheryl frowned. "Not exactly. But I'd think the old Calloway property would be a good starting place. I just have to find out where that is."

He nodded. "Promise me you won't go searching for Gary or the gold alone."

"Of course."

"Before I forget—here are the Bible covers I made." He handed them to her. "I will go to the farm and pick up Maam, Daed, Caleb, and Esther. They are going to join the search party. We have several neighbors who will be there too."

"I called Kathy Snyder on my walk to work this morning and let her know. She's bringing several volunteers too and is going to stop in area businesses this morning and let them know we'll be meeting here this afternoon. Can you be here in about an hour?"

He nodded. "In the meantime, call Chief Twitchell. He needs to know what you have discovered."

"I will."

Levi nodded and left the store.

Cheryl tucked the riddle into her purse for safekeeping. She couldn't wait to tell Lynn what she'd figured out. But she'd better call the chief first. She picked up her phone to dial his number, but the bell over the front door jingled.

She'd forgotten to lock up behind Levi.

She looked up, and an older man stood in the doorway. "Are you open?" he asked.

"Yes, sir." She may as well make a sale. Her call to the chief could wait a few minutes.

He strode down the aisle, a smile on his weathered face. "You must be Cheryl," he said. He was a hefty man, and between that and his white hair and beard, he reminded Cheryl of a mall Santa.

She furrowed her brow. "I'm sorry. Have we met?" His face did look kind of familiar, particularly the eyes. But she was pretty sure she'd never met him.

He let out a rumbling laugh. "Not officially." He stuck out a hand. "I'm Mr. Arnold. I'm sponsoring the treasure hunt."

She widened her eyes. "I'm glad to finally meet you." She shook his hand. "The event is so much fun. Lori is great." She knew how much Lori always seemed to want to please her boss, so maybe a few kind words about her would help. "Are you here for the final week of the hunt?"

"I sure am. I hate that I've missed all the gatherings up to this point, but I'll be there Thursday for the big finale."

Cheryl nodded. "That's wonderful. I know all the participants will be glad to hear from you."

He motioned toward the old volume of Sugarcreek history that she'd left on the counter. "That looks like an old book."

"It needs to be returned to the library. I think it's pretty old."

Mr. Arnold reached out and took the book then flipped through it. "Old books always smell the same, don't they?"

Cheryl began to feel uneasy. What was he doing here? "Is there something I can help you with? I was just getting ready to close up for lunch. I have a few errands to run."

"I just wanted to stop in and meet you." He glanced around. "Seems like everyone else thinks the store is closed. Are your employees at lunch?"

Her instincts told her something was wrong. "Yeah, but they should be back soon. Like, any minute." Her voice cracked. "Do you know what time it is?"

Mr. Arnold whipped out a pocket watch and checked the time.

She stared in horror at the watch. The ornate pocket watch.

Jimmy.

Their eyes met, and in that instant, she knew that he knew his cover was blown.

# CHAPTER TWENTY-EIGHT

There's nothing to be nervous about," Jimmy said in a low voice. "I have no interest in harming you."

"What do you want?"

"You know exactly what I want. I want what was in that book."

Would playing dumb help or hurt in this situation? She was about to find out. "What are you talking about?"

He pounded on the counter. "The map," he hissed. "I know the map was in the book. Gary told me that's where he stowed it."

She shook her head. "I don't have it." That was true. She didn't have it here. She had watched enough movies to know that as long as the bad guy thought you had something they wanted, your odds were pretty good. It was when you no longer held knowledge they needed that you were in trouble.

"Don't lie to me." The resemblance to Santa was gone. Now he just reminded her of a lunatic.

"I'm not. The map is not here. I'm sorry." If she could just stall for a bit longer, the volunteers would come in to help search for Gary.

He regarded her for a moment that felt like an hour. "Here's how this is gonna work," he growled. "You are going to do exactly as I say."

She sized him up. As soon as they got to the door, she could make a run for it.

"Don't think about running." Jimmy pulled a gun from his pocket and aimed it right at Cheryl.

She gasped. "I'm not. Look. I—I really don't have the map. It's not in the book. You know that. I can't help you."

"Oh, but I think you can." He grabbed the book from the counter and kept the gun on her. "Here's how this is gonna go. You are gonna walk out in front of me. If you scream, squeal, run, or try to draw attention to us, you will regret it. Do I make myself clear?"

"Yes."

"Good girl. Now walk to the door. When you get outside, keep walking until you see a silver Honda Accord. Get in the passenger side, and don't say a word."

She swallowed hard. Not exactly how she'd expected the day to turn out. She walked down the aisle of the Swiss Miss, hoping a customer or a friend would choose that moment to come by.

No such luck.

With each step, Cheryl's knees threatened to buckle. She opened the door and stepped outside into the bright sunshine. It looked like a normal day. She saw people around, running errands on their lunch breaks. But that didn't help her any.

"The car is straight ahead. The passenger side is unlocked. Go get inside," Jimmy growled.

Once they were inside, he looked over at her. "Keep following my directions, and you'll be fine. I don't want to hurt anyone."

Even though pulling a gun and taking someone hostage didn't give him much credibility, she believed him for some reason. "Okay."

They drove to the outskirts of Sugarcreek and turned down a dirt road. "Was this your family farm?"

He nodded. "Yes." He motioned. "Now, get out and no funny business."

She did what she was told. "Where are we going?"

"I found a hideout on the old property." He motioned toward a clearing. "Now go."

They reached what looked like an old cellar door.

"I uncovered this last week when I was searching for the gold. It made for a perfect hideout."

He unlocked the door and opened it. "You go first, and I'll shine the light for you."

"You want me to climb down those rickety stairs?" She could only see the top two stairs, but she could tell they were old and not so sturdy.

"Do it."

Cheryl turned around and held on to the railing as she descended into the darkness. The air was cool and musty.

Jimmy shone a flashlight for her, but the darkness was barely breached.

"Who is there?" a male voice said.

"Cheryl. Cheryl Cooper."

The man groaned. "Jimmy is such an idiot. What was he thinking?"

She reached the bottom of the stairs and waited for her eyes to adjust to the dimly lit space. There was a lantern on the wall that gave an eerie glow. "Mr. Calloway?" she asked.

Gary nodded. "Yep." He held up his wrists. "I'm all tied up, so I'm of no help."

The door at the top closed, and a moment later Jimmy reached the bottom. "I guess you two know each other."

Cheryl and Gary both nodded.

"If you'll just cooperate, this will go much faster," Jimmy began. "Gary told me the map was in that library book. I went to his room to find it, but it was gone."

So that explained the ransacking.

"I called Lynn this morning pretending to be the librarian looking for it, and she told me that you had it. And you did." He glared. "But the map was gone."

Cheryl shook her head. "I don't have it with me. I'm sorry."

"I'm not," said Gary. "I'm glad. Jimmy doesn't deserve it."

"Oh, like you do?"

"I never would've kidnapped you to get your map. And I sure wouldn't have gotten an innocent girl involved. You've gone too far, Jimmy, and you know it." Gary shook his head.

Cheryl looked around at her surroundings. "What is this place anyway?"

"It seems to be some kind of old root cellar," said Gary.

Cheryl's eyes grew wide. They were in the location. They were in the root cellar on the old Calloway property. But neither cousin knew this was the place because they had never been able to put the riddle together. She watched them argue.

Now was not the time to tell them. She was sure of it. Things may only escalate if they found out they might only be a few inches from their buried family treasure.

"What's your plan, Jimmy?" Gary asked. "Or do you have one?"

Jimmy glowered at his cousin. "We're going to wait a bit, and then she's going to take me to the map." He pointed at Cheryl. "I saw those Amish brothers though, and I don't want them getting suspicious."

"What Amish brothers?" Cheryl asked.

"The Stoltz brothers. From the treasure hunt. Haven't you figured out yet that this game was partly rigged?" Gary asked. "Jimmy was behind the whole thing. He contacted me early on when the hunt began. He was hoping I'd share my half of the riddle with him and he'd be able to use that in the competition. So he only wanted the best of the best in the final five. He wanted you because you have a reputation for solving puzzles. The Stoltz brothers' property shares some land with what used to be our family land. The Vogels are older, and he thought they might be useful. The Mennonite couple is smart and seemed capable, plus James knows the lay of the land pretty well."

"So who were the actual top five?"

Gary chuckled. "That's what is so funny. The people Jimmy handpicked as wanting to be sure were in the top five were the actual teams who made it in. So he didn't even have to stoop to low measures to get things to go his way."

"Did you want us to find the gold?" Cheryl asked.

Jimmy shook his head. "Not really. It occurred to me that if I could get Gary's half of the riddle, I could use that as one of your clues just to see what you all came up with. But I mainly wanted people going around Sugarcreek hunting for clues. That way I could hunt for the family gold and have a cover. Anytime anyone saw me out searching, I just told them I was part of the treasure hunt." He looked pleased with himself. "It was the perfect cover."

"How did he lure you away from your hotel?" she asked Gary.

Gary groaned. "That was my own dumb fault. I should've known better. But Lynn and I got separate clues at the library. Mine said to meet in front of the hotel by a silver Honda, and I'd get the next clue. I didn't realize it was a trap until it was too late."

"And I overheard the two of you talking the day we found the depot clue."

Jimmy nodded. "He was trying to act like he was closing in on the location of the gold. I didn't believe him." He smiled. "And as usual, I was right." He chuckled.

"How about Lori?" Cheryl asked. "Was she in on it too?"

For the first time, Jimmy looked remorseful. "She was one of my graduate assistants at the university. She had no idea that I had a connection to the area or that I wasn't who I said I was. I've used my middle name and my mother's maiden name during my whole professional career, so she's only ever known me as Mr. Andrew Arnold. I hate to have betrayed her, and I sure hated knowing how upset she was when I put out those flyers and switched out the library clue cards. I only did that to try to get Gary away from the group."

The whole thing was beginning to make sense now.

"Okay. Enough talking. It's time to take me to the map." He motioned toward Cheryl. "Same as before. No funny business. You march right up those stairs and push the door open. When you get to the top, stay there. Remember that I have a gun pointed at you. You may be able to outrun me, but you can't outrun a bullet."

He had a point.

She glanced at Gary. "You'll be okay. I guess we'll be back soon."

"Don't give him the map," Gary pleaded.

Cheryl didn't know that she had a choice. She started up the steep stairs, holding on to the rail and praying the entire time. She reached the top and pushed it open.

When her head was above ground, she glanced around.

The whole place was surrounded by police. Chief Twitchell held a finger to his lips, indicating she shouldn't give them away.

She spotted Levi behind the police, and he locked eyes with her.

Relief washed over her.

She was going to be okay.

# Chapter Twenty-Nine

A re you sure you're fine?" Levi asked. "Do you need to go to the hospital or anything?" He motioned toward the ambulance. EMTs were loading Gary inside.

Cheryl shook her head. "I'm fine. I'm just glad you figured out where I was being held."

He grinned. "Me too. I went back to the Swiss Miss, and it was unlocked. I saw your notes on the counter. I knew you wouldn't have gone anywhere when we were supposed to meet at your store. I called the police and let them know what you had figured out. They were already closing in on the location. The Stoltz brothers had noticed some suspicious activity out at their place as well. When it turned out their land and the old Calloway land was one and the same, it made sense to search here. We saw Jimmy's car parked some distance from here, so we knew this was the right location."

She'd never wanted to hug anyone more in her whole life. Instead she just smiled. "I can't thank you enough."

Chief Twitchell sauntered over. "Ms. Cooper, I know I normally reprimand you for getting involved in these sorts of things, but from what I know of this situation, you weren't here of your own accord."

"No, sir. In fact, I was just about to call you when Jimmy got to the store. I definitely didn't want to be involved."

"Very good. I'm glad you're safe."

"Thanks."

Naomi and Seth came over to where she stood. Naomi gave her a hug. "We were worried. I am glad the situation is over."

"Me too." Her eyes filled with tears. She'd been more scared than she'd let on. "I think I'm ready to go home and put this day behind me."

"Sounds like a goot idea," Seth said. "We will take you home."

"Esther and I will open the store tomorrow," Naomi said as they approached Cheryl's house. "Why not take the day off to recover?"

Cheryl's eyes filled with tears again. "Thank you. That's very kind."

"We do not mind at all."

"Do you still want to try to find the final clue?" Levi asked.

"What? Oh yes. That's tomorrow afternoon." She nodded. "I'll come to the store around four thirty. Naomi, you and Esther can go help us find it if you'd like."

Naomi beamed. "I think that sounds like fun."

Cheryl had never been so happy to see her house. She waved bye to the Millers and thanked them for their assistance then went inside.

Julia and Beau were on the couch, waiting. Julia jumped up. "I'm glad to see you!" she exclaimed. "They told me to wait here in case you called or something." She gave Cheryl a big hug. "Are you okay?"

"I am now." She would be fine. Now that she knew Jimmy's gun had been fake and she'd never been in real danger, she was much more at ease. "I think I'll take a hot bath and go to bed though."

"I don't blame you." Julia smiled. "And by the way, I called my parents. They'll be arriving on Friday. I'm going to come clean to them and tell them the truth about everything."

Cheryl nodded. "I think that's a great idea. I'll be around if you need me to talk to them on your behalf or if I can do anything to help you." She reached down and gave Beau a pat then headed to the bathroom. A hot bubble bath was calling her name, followed by a full night's sleep.

The next morning, she awoke to a message from Chief Twitchell. She needed to come down to the station and give a statement.

She got ready quickly and drove to the police station.

"Cheryl, thanks for comin'." The chief met her at the door. "This won't take long."

She went over what had transpired the previous day until they were both satisfied.

"Jimmy Calloway, aka Mr. Andrew Arnold, has asked to speak to you. I told him that would be up to you though."

She nodded. "It's okay. I don't mind hearing what he has to say." She followed Chief Twitchell down a long hallway.

He stopped in front of a door that had a window at the top. "You'll be behind glass. I think it will help him if you'll hear him out though."

Cheryl went inside and sat down in the chair.

Jimmy walked in and sat down across from her on the other side of the glass. He motioned for her to pick up the phone receiver.

She held it to her ear.

"I want to apologize for scaring you the way I did." He shook his head. "There is no excuse for the things I've done. I let my hate and my greed get so out of control that it's ruled my whole life up until now."

Cheryl didn't know what to say, but she suspected just listening might be enough for him.

"I know an apology doesn't change what happened, but I want you to know I am genuinely sorry."

"I forgive you."

He managed a small smile. "Thank you. That means a lot." He furrowed his brow. "And if I may give you some advice, it would be this: put your focus on the things that matter. I didn't do that. If I had, my life may have turned out completely different."

She nodded. "I will be praying for you to find the peace you need."

The old man's eyes filled with tears. "Thank you."

She gave him a tiny wave and went to find the chief. "What will happen to him now?"

"He'll definitely do some time. He kidnapped his cousin and held him against his will overnight. Not to mention holdin' you up at gunpoint, albeit with a fake gun." He shrugged. "I think there are likely some underlying issues goin' on with him though and that might make his sentence easier. We'll just have to wait and see. I will share with you that he's asked his cousin and his wife to come see him. Gary is in the hospital bein' treated for dehydration—he'll be fine, it was just a precaution. I suspect they will come here when he is released."

"Thanks for the information." It wasn't like the chief to share inside information with her, so that must mean he was still feeling sorry for her having gone through a frightening experience.

She drove home and found a note from Julia waiting. She'd gone for a drive so she could practice what she was going to say to her parents on Friday. Cheryl smiled. That was exactly the sort of thing she did when she had to tell someone something important.

Her phone dinged as an e-mail came through.

Aunt Mitzi.

Dear Cheryl,

I'm online right now. If you get this message and are able, try to reach me via Skype. If you aren't able to right now, try again tomorrow morning before you leave for work.

Love always,
Aunt Mitzi

Cheryl opened her laptop and connected to Skype. A moment later, Aunt Mitzi's smiling face appeared on the screen.

"Hi, dear." Aunt Mitzi waved. "I thought I might catch you at home for lunch."

Cheryl shook her head. "Not exactly." She took a deep breath and gave Mitzi the short version of the previous day's events.

Aunt Mitzi's eyes grew wide. "Oh my! I'm so thankful you're safe." She grinned. "And how romantic that Levi saved the day."

Cheryl felt her face turn three shades of red. "The police were there too."

"Of course they were, dear." Aunt Mitzi gave her a knowing stare.

It was time to change the topic. "How is your friend Ted?"

Now it was Aunt Mitzi's turn to blush. "He's fine. Just fine." She giggled. "It's like I always say, sixty is the new forty."

Cheryl grinned. It was nice to see her aunt so happy. She'd save the grilling on the status of her and Ted's relationship for another day.

"I'd better go now, dear." Aunt Mitzi gave her another little wave. "I love you, and I pray for you daily."

"You too."

They disconnected, and Cheryl closed the laptop.

Later that afternoon, Cheryl drove to the Swiss Miss. Levi, Naomi, and Esther were all waiting when she arrived.

They piled in the car.

"Are you feeling okay today?" Naomi asked. "Are you sure you are up to hunting this clue? We can do it for you if you would like."

Cheryl smiled. "Thanks for being concerned. I feel fine. I feel very thankful and blessed that yesterday turned out the way it did. It could have gone a much different way."

"I have been thanking Gott for your safety, Cheryl," said Naomi. "You gave us quite a scare."

"Let's talk about something else, shall we? How about the next clue?" Cheryl took the clue from her purse. "Here it is again:

> "You've all searched low.
> You've all searched high.
> And now it's time
> to say good-bye.
> At the final stop
> there are no dragons.
> It's where you go
> to ride a wagon."

"I am afraid I have no ideas." Levi shook his head. "I am stumped."

Esther cleared her throat from the backseat. "I think I may know."

Cheryl turned around to look at her. "Where?"

"How about the Farm at Walnut Creek?" Esther asked. "There are no dragons, but they have almost every other kind of animal. And they offer wagon rides a few times a day. That's how you go around to feed the animals."

"That's brilliant!" Cheryl exclaimed. "Let's give it a shot."

She drove the short distance to the Farm at Walnut Creek and finally turned down the long driveway that led to the barn where visitors checked in. She parked, and they all got out of the car.

"But where would it be hidden?" Cheryl asked.

"What about the wagon?" Levi pointed toward the large wagon that would hold many visitors on one of the tours. "That seems like the logical place to me."

Fifteen minutes later, they got back in the Ford Focus. "I can't believe that was the last one," Cheryl said. "Did you notice that this time there was no logbook to sign?"

Naomi nodded. "There must have been a camera on us that will tell them the order in which we arrived."

"Even if we do not win the prize, I think it has been a lot of fun," Levi said. "The clues have been interesting, and this activity has helped us see Sugarcreek in a different light. I guess Cheryl probably sees it that way since she has only been here a short time—but I think I definitely appreciate our home more now."

Cheryl pulled into a parking space near where the Millers' horse and buggy was parked. "Will you all be at the closing ceremony tomorrow night?"

"We would not miss it," Naomi said.

# Chapter Thirty

Cheryl woke up Thursday morning feeling like a new woman. She'd gotten a lot of sleep since her ordeal and felt great. She got dressed and went to the kitchen to grab a bite to eat.

"Good morning," Julia said. She stood in front of the stove, an oven mitt on her hand. "I'm just waiting for the timer."

"What are you timing?" Cheryl asked.

"A delicious spinach and cheese quiche. I got some farm-fresh eggs at the produce stand yesterday. They were gorgeous blues and dark browns. I'll bet they taste amazing too."

The timer went off, and Julia pulled the quiche out of the oven.

"Looks good." Cheryl took two plates from the cabinet.

Once they were seated, Cheryl took a bite. "This is very good. If the restaurant you own someday serves breakfast, you'll need to put this on the menu."

Julia laughed. "That's jumping the gun a little. I think I will have to start at the low end of things first." She still looked pleased though.

"When will your parents get here?"

"Tomorrow morning. We're going to meet up for breakfast at the Honey Bee Café, and then I'll show them around. Then we'll come back here and talk."

Cheryl took a sip of juice. "Are you nervous?"

Julia nodded. "Very. But I'm also relieved. Keeping such a big secret from them has been killing me. I think a huge part of me has known all along that I'd never go through with going to OSU. But just finding the nerve to tell them my plans has been difficult. So thanks for pushing me to get to that place."

"And what are your plans? Do you have one?" Cheryl put her plate and fork in the dishwasher and finished off her juice.

"I'm going to ask Mom and Dad if I can live at home for the next few months and get some basics at a local community college. I'll try to get a job in the kitchen of a restaurant too and save the money so I can pay for culinary school."

It seemed like a logical and well-thought-out plan. Whether Michelle and Jared agreed would be another story. "Do you want me to be here while you talk to them? Or do you want to bring them by the Swiss Miss afterward?"

"I think I'll try to do this alone. And maybe when we come see you, you can tell them what a great chef you think I'll be someday." She grinned. "They don't really eat much of the stuff I cook."

"I'll certainly do that." Cheryl grinned. "I'll tell them if you lived nearby I'd sell your baked goods in the store."

Cheryl grabbed her bag and called Beau. "Don't worry about cooking dinner tonight. It's the wrap-up party."

Julia widened her eyes. "I didn't know if they'd have it since the guy behind the whole thing is in jail."

"He insisted. I guess the prize money had already been set aside and the catering bill paid. So why not go through with the contest?" She shrugged. "I wonder if Lori will acknowledge it though."

"No telling." Julia cut a small sliver of quiche and put it on her plate. "But I'll be ready when you get home."

Cheryl tossed her bag over her shoulder and picked up Beau's carrier. Today was going to be a good day. She just knew it.

By lunchtime, Cheryl was back in the groove. Esther had come in midmorning and helped her handle two tour groups, and things were finally starting to slow down again.

The bell jingled, and Lynn and Gary walked into the store holding hands. Maybe kidnapping was good for rekindling a relationship.

"I'm glad to see you up and around, Mr. Calloway. How are you feeling?"

He smiled. "I'm well. How about you?"

"Fine." She turned to Lynn. "I guess you're happy to have your other half back."

Lynn beamed. "I sure am." She grew serious. "We came to ask you something, Cheryl."

Cheryl froze. She'd returned the map yesterday and had also taken the library book back. "What's wrong?"

"We wanted to ask you to go with us to locate the Calloway family treasure," said Gary. "You were so nice to Lynn—a friend when she needed one the most. You tried to reason with Jimmy, and he told us this morning that you'd forgiven him. Besides, you're the one who figured out the location of the gold after all."

A real live treasure hunt? She couldn't turn it down. "Okay. Just let me tell Esther I'll be out for a little while."

Twenty minutes later they were back at the root cellar entrance. "I guess Jimmy must've been pretty heartbroken to realize he'd been in the right location all along—even without your half of the clue."

"He was. But really, I think Jimmy will come out of the whole experience a better man. I know I will," said Gary. "There's no reason we should've let things fester as long as we did."

Cheryl was glad to hear him say that. She hoped everyone involved had learned a lesson. "Okay, who wants to go first?"

"I'm going to throw the shovels down first," Gary said. "Then I'll go if someone will hold the light."

The three of them carefully descended into the root cellar. It was just as it had been on Tuesday—damp, dark, and musty.

"Any idea where to look? Did Jimmy ever let you see his map?"

Lynn nodded. "He gave it to us. The only thing he asked was that we take photos of the treasure and whatever may be with it."

"From what I could tell on the map, the thing they had in common was a symbol. I believe it was the family crest." He shone the light around the cellar. "If we can find that symbol, we'll have our digging spot."

Cheryl used her phone's flashlight app to search the back wall. On a whim, she turned the light upward. "There it is!" she exclaimed. Gary and Lynn hurried to her side and each directed their flashlight at the spot on the ceiling.

"Maybe directly underneath?" Lynn asked.

Gary grabbed a shovel. "Let's find out."

It took the three of them the better part of an hour to dig up the old chest.

"The handles still look pretty sturdy," said Cheryl. "Do you think we can manage to get it out of the cellar?"

"If we go slowly."

Cheryl took one end and Gary took the other, while Lynn held the light. They carefully made their way up the rickety stairs and out into the sunlight then put the trunk down.

Lynn snapped a few photos. "Open it, Gary. You've been waiting your whole life for this moment."

He unlatched the front of the trunk and swung it open.

The three of them peered inside.

It may not have been a fortune worth of gold, but it was enough. "Wow," Gary whispered. "I wish my dad were here to see this." He reached inside and pulled out an envelope. "Look here. It's addressed to Walt and Simon." He carefully opened the envelope while Lynn photographed the inside of the trunk.

Darling Walt and Simon,

When you read this, your papa and I will be long gone. You brought us such joy when you were youngsters. More importantly, you loved each other so much. We have grieved as we've stood by and watched you drift apart—even watched you lash out at one another. It is our hope that by coming together to find your inheritance, you will also put your differences in the past. You may believe the treasure in this trunk is in the form of gold nuggets. But that is not so. The truest treasures aren't made of gold or silver. They are the people around you and the love you have in your heart.

> With all our love, now and forever,
> Mother and Papa

The three of them stood in silence. "That's so sad." Cheryl shook her head. "If only Walt and Simon had been the ones to open this trunk the way William and Lola meant for them to, so many lives would've turned out differently."

"All we can do is live differently now," said Gary. "And that's what we will do."

They loaded up the trunk and drove back into town.

And just like that, after more than a century underground, the Calloway gold was located.

Cheryl was thrilled to have been a part of it.

# CHAPTER THIRTY-ONE

So how much gold was it?" Kathy Snyder asked as they filed into the bleachers for the wrap-up party.

"They won't be rich because of it, but it will provide them with a comfortable retirement. Although Gary says he's putting half of it up for Jimmy so he can have it when he's released."

"That's the way it should be," said Julia. "I'm glad he is going to share."

Cheryl pointed to two seats below the Miller family. "Hi, everyone," she said as she sat down.

"Thanks for coming, ladies and gentleman," Lori said from the front podium. "I think we've all heard that there's been an awful lot of excitement surrounding the treasure hunt and all the goings on behind the scenes." She grinned. "I want to assure everyone that the top five teams were in fact the top five teams. There was no cheating or manipulating the results. That's one thing I can speak for." She cleared her throat. "The other thing I can speak for is that my boss is going to honor his promise of a one-thousand-dollar prize. He may have made some poor choices lately, but deep down he's a good man, and he actually does care very deeply about geocaching and treasure hunts. It's ironic though. I think by now we've heard of his circumstance—estranged from family and on his own for the most part. But the reason he loves these hunts so much is because he thinks it brings family close together."

The crowd applauded.

"I won't speak long. You've all been a wonderful crowd, and we've had some really fun participants. But it's time to name the winner of the Sugarcreek Treasure Hunt." She took an envelope from the podium and opened it. "The winner of the one-thousand-dollar prize is . . . James and Grace Ladd."

James and Grace jumped up and ran down to the front.

Lori presented them with a check, and they turned to face the crowd.

"I'm really glad for them," said Julia. "Because look how happy they are."

Grace and James did seem to be full of pure joy. Cheryl wouldn't doubt if they didn't give a portion of the money to the church or to a family in need.

"Congratulations to James and Grace and a special thank-you to all those who participated. I debated sharing this, but I think everyone will like to know—there was a less than five-minute difference in first and second place. All our teams did a great job. Let's give them all a hand."

The crowd clapped.

"I hope you'll all stay and eat and visit," Lori said. "There's plenty of food, and it smells delicious."

She dismissed them, and the crowd headed toward the food line. "Let us go say congratulations to James and Grace," said Levi.

Cheryl nodded and followed him down to where they stood.

Grace pulled Cheryl into a hug. "I'm so glad to have met you and Levi," she said. "Please keep in touch." She leaned forward and whispered, "And if you ever decide to visit our church, give me a call. We're in the book."

Cheryl grinned. "Of course." She made her way over to where Julia and Esther stood talking. "Let's go get in line, girls."

They followed her to the line, and she glanced around at the crowd. Kathy Snyder stood talking to Ben Vogel and laughed at something he said. Naomi and Seth were visiting with Ray and Marion Berryhill, the owners of the By His Grace bookstore. Levi and James were locked in a discussion about something, but it was punctuated with laughter.

She couldn't help but think of the letter William and Lola had left for their sons. What they'd said still held true today— relationships with family and friends meant more than any treasure money could buy.

And Cheryl was blessed to be a part of a community of people who understood the value of those relationships.

The next morning, Julia was already gone when Cheryl got up. "Beau, it's about to just be you and me again. Hope that won't be too boring for you." He purred and wound around her legs.

She got ready for work and headed out the door. The excitement of the last couple of weeks had been fun, but she was looking forward to a Friday night at home, kicking back with a good book or maybe even a cheesy movie.

As soon as she arrived at the Swiss Miss, she let Beau out of his carrier and put some coffee on to brew. It would be nice to be back to her daily routine.

She'd just poured herself a cup of coffee when the door opened. Julia, Michelle, and Jared walked inside.

She tried to read their expressions. Julia had planned to talk to her parents before they came to the Swiss Miss. But no one looked especially angry, so maybe she'd chickened out.

"Cheryl, I can't thank you enough for letting Julia stay with you for these past couple of weeks," Michelle said. "She seems to have really had a great time here—and definitely done some good thinking."

Cheryl raised an eyebrow in Julia's direction.

Julia nodded. "I told them everything." The stress that had been on her earlier was gone, and she looked like a carefree teenage girl. "They were a little hesitant at first."

Michelle snorted. "A little? We were a lot hesitant. It's hard to hear that the life you thought your baby girl wanted wasn't what she wanted at all." She shook her head. "I just thought all the things she was mentioning were nerves. I guess I didn't really hear her until she sat us down and talked to us like she was an adult." She pulled Julia to her. "And I guess she is."

Julia blushed.

"I'm glad you were able to get it worked out. So what's the plan now?"

Julia and her mom exchanged a glance. "It's just like I mentioned. I'll live at home this semester and take some basics at a community college. But my main focus will be finding a job quickly in a restaurant, hopefully in the kitchen. Working and living at home will let me save up money to help pay for culinary school." She was positively glowing.

"I'm so happy to hear that everyone is on the same page about things," Cheryl said.

"Mind if I look around a little bit?" Jared asked. "That bread over there looks amazing."

"Sure. And you're going to want to get a jar of those preserves too." Cheryl grinned.

Michelle wrinkled her nose. "I try not to keep any kind of homemade bread in the house. We don't seem to have as much willpower as we used to."

"Well if you'll let Julia cook some meals for you, you won't even care about having willpower. Although you may need to build a gym in your house."

"Dad, you have to look at these Amish dolls," Julia said as she went to join Jared.

"I have to say, I wasn't quite sure what to expect when Julia told me she wanted to come stay with you," Michelle said. "But I'm really glad she did. I don't know what your future plans are, Cheryl, but you would make a fantastic mother someday."

Cheryl widened her eyes. "Well, thanks. I'd like to think I would if the timing was ever right." She definitely hoped for children someday, but there was no telling what might be in store for her.

Soon it was time for Julia and her parents to leave.

"Thanks so much for everything," Julia whispered as she hugged Cheryl good-bye. "If it wasn't for you, I think I'd be in the car on the way to OSU right now wishing I were anywhere else."

"I'm glad I could help. Text me sometime. I want to know how your semester is going." She grinned. "And I especially want to know when you head to culinary school. I've always wanted to visit France."

Julia smiled. "Definitely."

She followed them out to the sidewalk and waved until their car was out of sight.

The store was quiet when she walked back in. She tidied up the counter and then sat down to make a list. The holidays would be here before long, and she needed to be sure she had the right inventory. Fudge was always popular and so were Christmas ornaments.

The bell over the door jingled, and Cheryl looked up.

Levi stepped inside, a smile on his handsome face. "I had to drive past and thought I had better stop by to make sure you had recovered completely from the week."

"I think so." She settled on the stool at the counter. "Being held up at gunpoint was definitely not my favorite way to spend an afternoon."

He nodded. "When did you realize the gun was not real?"

"I didn't know that until Chief Twitchell told me after the whole thing was over."

"Were you scared?" he asked softly.

"At first I was. But then when we got to the root cellar and Gary and Jimmy started arguing about every little thing, I started to see that they were really like two wounded little boys. That family has held on to so much anger and resentment. It mostly just made me sad for them. And visiting Jimmy in jail was pretty pitiful. He's getting toward the end of his life, and he is all alone."

She shook her head. "I just kept thinking how I didn't want that to be me."

Levi looked surprised. "I do not think you have anything to worry about there. Haven't you noticed that your life is very full of people who care about you?"

"I just recently realized that. I think that's a fear I can finally let go of."

He grinned. "I had better get back to the farm. Have a nice weekend, Cheryl."

"You too."

She watched as he walked out the door.

He was right. Her life was full of people—people she cared for and people who cared for her.

This was a good life. A blessed life.

A life she was thankful for each and every day.

# Author Letter

Dear Reader,

I hope you enjoyed another glimpse into Cheryl's life in Sugarcreek, Ohio. It's such fun to collaborate on this series, and I hope by now you're eagerly anticipating the next book so you can see what's going on with Cheryl and her friends.

As for me, I always appreciate the chance to step back into Sugarcreek. I have such fond memories of the area from my visits, and it seems like each time I write a book set there, I learn something new about the town.

Thanks so much for reading!

Blessings,
Annalisa Daughety

# ABOUT THE AUTHOR

Annalisa Daughety is the best-selling author of more than fifteen novels and novellas including the series Walk in the Park, *A Wedding to Remember in Charleston*, and *Love Finds You in Charm, Ohio*, which was made into a movie for UP TV. She writes contemporary stories set in historic locations and classifies her writing style as romantic comedy.

Annalisa lives in Arkansas with her husband, Johnny, and when she's not working or writing, she enjoys raising chickens, gardening, and traveling. She loves connecting with readers on Facebook, Twitter, Instagram, and Pinterest. Find more information about her at annalisadaughety.com.

# Fun Fact about
# the Amish or Sugarcreek, Ohio

I last visited Sugarcreek during the filming of *Love Finds You in Charm*, which was based on a Guideposts book that I authored. One of the locations used for the movie was Sweetwater Farms. In the movie, it was the storefront for Lydia Ann's farm stand. In reality, Sweetwater Farms is a real produce stand with wonderful locally grown fruits and vegetables as well as jams and preserves. In the fall, they also have a beautiful selection of mums, pumpkins, and gourds.

When I wrote Julia's storyline in *Earthly Treasures*, I knew Sweetwater Farms was a place she needed to visit. Her character enjoys cooking with fresh, local ingredients—and Sweetwater Farms was the perfect place for that.

# SOMETHING DELICIOUS FROM OUR SUGARCREEK FRIENDS

## *Julia's Honey Pumpkin Pie*

3 eggs

2 cups pumpkin puree

¾ cup heavy whipping cream

½ cup honey

1½ teaspoons ground cinnamon

1 teaspoon pumpkin pie spice

½ teaspoon salt

¼ cup sugar (optional)

Unbaked pie crust

Beat eggs in a large bowl. Blend in pumpkin, cream, honey, spices, salt, and sugar. Pour filling into pie shell.

Bake at four hundred degrees for fifty minutes.

Read on for a sneak peek of another exciting book
in the series Sugarcreek Amish Mysteries!

## *No Time for Trouble*
by Olivia Newport

Half the town was there. At least it seemed that way to
Cheryl Cooper as she leaned against the cool back wall at
the fire station. A young volunteer firefighter wagged his finger at
her.

"You can't stand back here," he said. "If we get a call, we need
to be able to get the engine out."

Cheryl would know to get out of the way of a revved-up fire
engine making a swift departure, but she saw his point. The chairs
set up for the occasion were in strictly arranged rows safely away
from the engine, and they all were occupied except for one seat in
the middle of the second to last row.

"Excuse me," Cheryl murmured as she squeezed past the knees
of four citizens of Sugarcreek. "Sorry. Excuse me."

The cold metal seat met the backs of her legs through her
khaki pants. After almost exactly a year in Sugarcreek, Cheryl was
still getting used to the bright blue color of the fire department's
equipment. Whatever happened to red fire trucks?

Mayor Clayton Weller stood at the front of the room shuffling papers—probably copies of the same documents he had distributed four times already. Every time the schedule of the Ohio Swiss Festival shifted by fifteen minutes, shop owners up and down Main Street received a revised edition. In her back room office at the Swiss Miss, Cheryl was careful to set aside outdated versions. Her neighbor twins could collect them for their recycling project. The festival was only a few days away, and the town had hosted it for more than sixty years. Surely not much would change at this point. But the mayor had summoned business owners, sponsoring organizations, and leaders of festival events, so Cheryl dutifully left the Swiss Miss in the capable hands of Lydia Troyer and Esther Miller and turned up at the fire station.

Gail Murray, owner of the Buttons 'n Bows shop down the street from the Swiss Miss, leaned her head toward Cheryl and whispered, "Clayton looks rattled."

Cheryl craned her neck for a better look at the mayor. In her mind, he always seemed distracted, but today was worse than usual.

She glanced around the room. Kathy Snyder, from the Honey Bee Café across the street from the Swiss Miss, sat between Jacob Hoffman from the furniture store and Marion Berryhill from By His Grace bookstore. August Yoder represented the popular Yoder's Corner restaurant. Brandon Richardson's veterinary practice was several miles off Main Street, but he was sponsoring a float for the Grand Parade. Cheryl's eyes finally settled on the people she always looked for at any town gathering—Naomi Miller, her husband Seth, and Levi. When Naomi married Seth, she became mother to his three young children, Levi, Caleb, and Sarah, before adding Eli, Elizabeth, and Esther to the family. On the schedules, Miller names were attached to a variety of festival activities—crafts, pastry stands, costumes, trolley tours, tents, judging, and a half dozen other entries in the mayor's master list. Naomi turned her head, and Cheryl caught her dark brown eyes and wiggled three fingers at her unlikely best friend. Naomi had been working the festival for more than two decades. Nothing would fluster her.

A year ago on festival weekend, Cheryl was occupied finishing up her move from Columbus in time to benefit from a couple of weeks of training from Aunt Mitzi, who owned the Swiss Miss, before Mitzi's departure for Papua New Guinea. Across the world, Aunt Mitzi was living her life's dream of missionary work. This was Cheryl's first time to see festival preparations in full swing, and every day the mayor's stress level notched up.

Cheryl intended to remain cool, calm, and collected. Tourists would throng to the town, and the shop would be extra busy, but she was ready. Lydia and Esther would both work full days during the festival, Kinsley Coleman was on call, and Cheryl had stocked up on additional inventory of her best-selling items. At the craft tent during the festival, Cheryl would find appealing items to mark up slightly and resell in the Swiss Miss.

Clayton Weller cleared his throat. "We have just a few details to update, and we'll have plenty of time for your questions."

Cheryl was right. Nothing the mayor said differed from information in the stapled papers he passed around town or the e-mail messages he sent to fifty inboxes on a daily basis. She jiggled a leg, and she wasn't the only one fidgeting. If the mayor didn't say something new soon, people would start leaving.

Two rows ahead of Cheryl, burly Melvin Hooley gripped the chair in front of him as he stood and then slid one thumb under a suspender. He adjusted his black felt hat. Instead of leaving, though, Melvin spoke—and spared no volume.

"Here is my question," Melvin said. "Why do we even want all these people to come to town in the first place?"

Cheryl's eyebrows rose.

"Sugarcreek has always been home to at least as many Plain People as *Englischers*, and we like to live simple." Melvin slapped the back of the chair before him, startling everyone in the row. "We do not need all this ruckus."

"It's a long-standing town tradition," the mayor said, his tired tone evidence that he had been around this loop with Melvin before. "No one is required to participate."

"Hooley cows have provided milk for the ice cream for forty years," Melvin said.

"And we appreciate it," the mayor said, "but if you prefer to pull out this year, you can speak to me privately and we will make other arrangements."

"The wife says I cannot do that," Melvin sputtered, his volume subsiding.

"Never mind the tourists." Another voice rose from across the room, and rows of heads turned toward Angus Krump. "We all know the cheese judging is rigged. I don't know why we go through the trouble of pretending it's a fair contest, when clearly the judges decide their favorite weeks before they taste the entries."

"You are grumpy because you do not win," Melvin Hooley said. "There is a reason the *kinder* call you Krump the Grump."

Krump shot out of his chair, his plaid shirt flashing through Cheryl's line of sight, and jabbed a finger toward Melvin. "You take that back."

"I will not. It is about time somebody started speaking the truth around here."

"Please, gentlemen." The mayor's conciliatory tone was nevertheless firm. "This is a treasured town tradition. Let's not turn it into something personal."

"Just speaking my mind," Melvin said.

"The judges are in cahoots." Angus pushed a fist into a palm. "There's not an honorable soul among them."

Cheryl seethed. Seth Miller was one of the cheese judges this year, and Sugarcreek didn't have a more honorable man than Seth.

"You're wrong, Mr. Krump." Cheryl had never spoken to Mr. Krump before, but she couldn't let his slanderous words go uncontested.

"Am not," Krump said.

"The judges are well qualified and above board." On her feet now, Cheryl's retort was firm. "It's wrong of you to speak that way about the judges."

"I will speak any way I choose. Maybe Hooley is right. It is time to tell the truth."

"Your truth or the real truth?" Cheryl glared.

Gail Murray tugged on Cheryl's arm and whispered, "Don't get sucked into this. Those two go at it every year."

Heat flushed Cheryl's face.

"Everyone, please!" Clayton Weller clapped his hands and stepped out from behind his podium. "This is not the time or place for these hostilities. This is an important time of year for the town to pull together. If you have a problem with the festival, speak to me or one of the committee members privately."

"Don't try to shut me up, Clayton," Krump snapped.

Naomi Miller raised her hand. Cheryl was back in her chair and wishing she had chosen the polite approach. Her impetuous outbursts rarely led to anything good, yet they persisted past every resolve to constrain them.

The mayor called on Naomi, and she stood.

"We are neighbors," she said. "Many of us have known each other since we were young. Our children have grown up together. The mayor is right that the festival is important to the town, but our friends Mr. Hooley and Mr. Krump are right that we want to be able to speak honestly with each other and be above reproach in all that we do. Perhaps we will serve each other well if we try to think the best of each other from the start and resolve our differences with gentleness."

"Our friend and neighbor Naomi has spoken well," the mayor said as Naomi sat down. "Good words to carry with us."

Mr. Krump slumped in his chair. To Cheryl he looked more chastised than repentant. Her own sharp words stung as they replayed in her mind. It wouldn't be easy, but she would have to apologize to Mr. Grump. *Krump*, she mentally corrected, though he deserved his nickname.

"I have a mind of my own, and I intend to use it." Rather than taking his seat, Melvin Hooley stomped out of the room. Relief rushed from every lung in the room.

"I've kept you all long enough," Clayton said. "If you have questions specific to your role in the festival, don't hesitate to ask me privately."

*Good move.* The mayor was right to contain the damage before it got worse. If only Cheryl could undo her contribution to the melee. As the assembly dispersed, Cheryl saw Naomi coming toward her.

"I'm sorry, I'm sorry," Cheryl said. "I should have kept my mouth shut. I just couldn't stand to hear anyone talk about Seth that way."

Naomi embraced her without speaking, and Cheryl's tense shoulders eased. Naomi's demeanor often had that affect on her. The longer Cheryl lived in Sugarcreek, the less she saw the differences between herself, with her busy city background, and Naomi and the Plain life among the Amish. But would she ever manage to take things in stride the way Naomi did?

They walked together toward the door. "Seth can hold his own," Naomi said. "Do not worry about him. The festival is important. A lot of people, both Amish and *Englisch*, depend on the income that comes in from the tourists, but there are so many details to take care of, and something always goes wrong."

"I just wish I hadn't contributed."

"You will make it right." Naomi looked over her shoulder at her husband and stepson. "Do you want to say hello to Seth and Levi?"

Cheryl puffed her cheeks and blew air out. Levi was at once both irresistible and circling her at a distance. After an entire year, Cheryl still did not know what to make of their interactions.

"I told the girls I would get back to the shop as quickly as I could," she said. "Lydia needs to leave on time."

"Then you should go." Naomi laid a hand on Cheryl's shoulder. "Send Esther down the street when it is convenient. We will be waiting for her here. Seth needs to speak to the other judges for a few minutes."

The heart of the Ohio Swiss Festival would be at the fire station, the nearby pavilion, and Midway in between. The Swiss Miss was farther west up Main Street, away from the intersection anchored by the fire station and the enormous cuckoo clock that celebrated Swiss culture every hour on the hour, but more than one business owner had assured her that the streets would be thick with tourists by Friday morning. Even the outlying shops would see brisk trade.

At the moment, Cheryl was glad for the distance. She needed more than a few yards of walking to settle her spirit and reclaim her resolution to remain cool, calm, and collected.

She reached the Swiss Miss, with its cream exterior accented in cornflower blue trim and red shutters. Her favorite feature, the turret on one side of the structure, stirred the imagination of the little girl inside her every time she saw it.

When Cheryl opened the shop door and ambled past the displays, Lydia and Esther were both busy with the last of the Saturday afternoon customers. In twenty minutes, Cheryl could turn the latch on the door and go home to enjoy a peaceful evening and a day off tomorrow.

Lydia rang up a sale, and Esther's customer, while grateful for information, left without making a purchase. As two cuckoo clocks on display announced the close of business, Cheryl shooed both girls away from their offers to help and turned the sign on the door to Closed. She emptied the cash register, tallied the day's sales, read three notes written in Esther's careful hand, prepared a bank deposit, and locked everything in the safe. Then she opened the bottom desk drawer and pulled out Aunt Mitzi's manila envelope.

*Do not open until Saturday before the festival.* For a year, Aunt Mitzi's familiar handwriting had taunted Cheryl, but she had abided by the clear instructions. Now the time had come. This was Saturday before the festival. She could read the envelope's contents over her supper.

# A Note from the Editors

We hope you enjoyed Sugarcreek Amish Mysteries, published by the Books and Inspirational Media Division of Guideposts, a nonprofit organization that touches millions of lives every day through products and services that inspire, encourage, help you grow in your faith, and celebrate God's love.

Thank you for making a difference with your purchase of this book, which helps fund our many outreach programs to military personnel, prisons, hospitals, nursing homes, and educational institutions.

We also create many useful and uplifting online resources. Visit Guideposts.org to read true stories of hope and inspiration, access OurPrayer network, sign up for free newsletters, download free e-books, join our Facebook community, and follow our stimulating blogs.

To learn about other Guideposts publications, including the best-selling devotional *Daily Guideposts*, go to Guideposts.org/Shop, call (800) 932-2145, or write to Guideposts, PO Box 5815, Harlan, Iowa 51593.

# Sign up for the
# Guideposts Fiction Newsletter
## *and stay up-to-date on the books you love!*

You'll get sneak peeks of new releases, recommendations from other Guideposts readers, and special offers just for you . . .

### *and it's FREE!*

## Just go to Guideposts.org/Newsletters
## today to sign up.

**Guideposts.**

Visit Guideposts.org/Shop
or call (800) 932-2145

# Find more inspiring fiction in these best-loved Guideposts series!

## Mysteries of Martha's Vineyard

Come to the shores of this quaint and historic island and dig into a cozy mystery. When a recent widow inherits a lighthouse just off the coast of Massachusetts, she finds exciting adventures, new friends, and renewed hope.

## Tearoom Mysteries

Mix one stately Victorian home, a charming lakeside town in Maine, and two adventurous cousins with a passion for tea and hospitality. Add a large scoop of intriguing mystery and sprinkle generously with faith, family, and friends, and you have the recipe for Tearoom Mysteries.

## Sugarcreek Amish Mysteries

Be intrigued by the suspense and joyful "aha!" moments in these delightful stories. Each book in the series brings together two women of vastly different backgrounds and traditions, who realize there's much more to the "simple life" than meets the eye.

## Mysteries of Silver Peak

Escape to the historic mining town of Silver Peak, Colorado, and discover how one woman's love of antiques helps her solve mysteries buried deep in the town's checkered past.

## Patchwork Mysteries

Discover that life's little mysteries often have a common thread in a series where every novel contains an intriguing whodunit centered around a quilt located in a beautiful New England town.

**To learn more about these books,
visit Guideposts.org/Shop**